CANYON OF THE DEAD

Canyon of the Dead

ANDREW McBRIDE

A Black Horse Western

ROBERT HALE · LONDON

ISBN 0 7090 5755 5

Robert Hale Limited
Clerkenwell House
Clerkenwell Green
London EC1R 0HT

Thanks again to P.D. and J.

Photoset in North Wales by
Derek Doyle & Associates, Mold, Clwyd.
Printed and bound in Great Britain by
WBC Book Manufacturers Limited,
Bridgend, Mid-Glamorgan.

ONE

Calvin Taylor woke instantly.

He listened.

Silence was thick in his ears. Not that the desert night was ever totally silent; but it was at its quietest now, in the darkest time. Taylor had to strain to hear distantly, the singing of a canyon wren. Gradually, he identified other sounds; the shuffling of hooves; horses stirring in the corral, thirty yards north.

Was it the horses' nervousness that had awakened him? Or were there men near the corral?

He reached through the darkness until he touched the barrel of the Winchester. There was some comfort in the chill of metal against his fingers. Especially if there *were* men near the horses. These men would be horsethieves. They might be white men or Apaches. It made no difference. Here, in Arizona Territory, horse-theft was the worst of all crimes; practitioners of the trade could expect only death and they'd be likely to respond in kind.

Taylor sat up. In a few minutes, he judged, false dawn would begin to show. He'd found it too hot to sleep indoors last night, instead he'd slept in the grounded wagon by the corral. He wore only longjohns and vest; now he pulled on his Apache moccasins, baggy deerskin boots that reached up over his knees. He buckled the gunbelt about his waist with the pistol, in its battered holster, against his right hip. He slid over the wagon tailgate, lowered himself noiselessly to earth, hoisted the Winchester after him and squatted under the wagon.

The valley floor was still in darkness. Taylor couldn't see any of the buildings – the barn, the adobe house – that made up the waystation of Coyote Springs. Nor could he see the horses, although he could hear them. They sneezed and coughed, stamping their feet. There were nine horses in the saddleband, mostly quarter horses, duns and paints, all of them riding stock and new to the saddle.

The stationhand, Dan Beckwirth, was bunking in the adobe, forty paces east of the corral. Almost certainly he would have noticed the disquiet of the stock. He'd be watching now, his 'Yellowboy' Winchester ready. Between them, Taylor and Beckwirth would have any horsethieves in a crossfire. They could turn the corral into a butcher's yard.

Thinking of that, Taylor felt his stomach tighten, but fear was already gouging him there. He felt dizzy with it, his throat fiercely dry. Don't do it, he told the horsethieves. It's not worth it, for just nine horses.

Dawn – a block of shining gold – was flushing the sky beyond the mountains. If there were men near the corral and if they were horsethieves, they'd have to move now, before full light. Already the dimness of the valley floor had faded from black to green. He began to detect movement, horses milling behind the corral bars. He stared at them until his eyes began to ache and just as he'd convinced himself he was staring at shadows, that there was nothing there, the pole barring the corral gate fell, ringing against the earth. The gate was flung wide and he heard a man yell at the top of his voice.

Taylor jammed the buttplate of his rifle into his shoulder, began to squeeze off a shot; Beckwirth fired first, from the bunkhouse. The horses started forward, boiling from the corral. The first swerved out through the gate. Taylor shot the second animal, putting it down in the gateway; the horses behind veered back, began to circle in the corral. They set up a fiendish screaming, ramming the mesquite bars. Taylor saw a man rear up against the sky, struggling to stay aboard a pitching horse. This would be the horsethief who'd sneaked into the corral, the daring one who'd thrown down the gate pole, herding the other horses before him. Taylor took a quick aim on him, fired and saw him knocked sideways; he fell amongst the horses.

Taylor levered the Winchester but the gloom before him was ripped apart in a blue explosion of flame. He ducked. The bullet struck the wagon bed above him. There was a dim shape running towards him. He took quick aim on the running man and squeezed the trigger. The dawn was rocked with a double concussion; the other man had fired at the same instant.

For a minute Taylor was deafened; he was blinded too, by the muzzle flash, then he heard the crazed whinnying of the horses in the corral. He blinked until he could see. Daylight was coming; he made out the corral, the waystation buildings, the mountains behind them. He saw a man lying thirty yards away, west of the corral. Taylor's bullet had spun him around, thrown him flat on his face. Now he sat up, one hand to his left shoulder.

Taylor stood. He walked towards the wounded man, halting ten paces from him. Taylor lifted his Winchester. He said, 'Keep still.' He spoke in Spanish. The horsethief looked like a *charro* – a Mexican cowboy – fallen on hard times, his leather jacket and trousers scuffed and whitened with dust. His straw sombrero had fallen from his head. There was blood all over the front of his shirt and jacket and he gasped with pain.

A rifle lay in the dust perhaps three yards away. *Charro* glanced over at the weapon, then at Taylor. He smiled. In Spanish he said, 'Better a bullet than a rope.'

Taylor nodded slowly. He said, 'If you feel that way, try for it.'

Charro thought about it; perhaps for a minute. Dan Beckwirth approached from the east, his Winchester in his hands. *Charro* stared at Beckwirth, then at Taylor. He shrugged.

Taylor found his arms were trembling.

Beckwirth declared, 'Jesus Christ, Taylor!'

Taylor said, 'Watch our friend here.' He walked over to the gun lying in the dust. It was a Spencer carbine, Civil War model, a good enough gun in its time but now, in the 1880s, ten years out of date. Taylor took the carbine by the barrel and smashed it against the wagon.

He told Beckwirth, 'Get a rope.'

'A rope?'

'I figger there's a dead man in the corral. Why those horses are still crazy.'

He roped the body in the corral and dragged it out from under the bars. Perhaps his shot had killed the man; he couldn't tell. There wasn't much he could tell about the horsethief, after the saddleband had kicked and trampled him to rags. Taylor asked Beckwirth, 'How about fixing some breakfast?'

'You had two men for breakfast!'

Beckwirth was barely twenty but his pale hair was receding already. A handlebar moustache aged his face. His fair skin gave him a lot of trouble under the Arizona sun. He glanced at the dead man uneasily. 'What about that corpse?'

'We'll plant him round sundown.'

'Why wait?'

'It'll be too hot, during the day, to dig graves.'

They buried the horsethief at sunset. Taylor and Beckwirth took turns digging. They'd placed some rocks on top of the dead man, to keep away wolves and other predators. They covered the rocks with earth. Their prisoner watched, his arm in the crude sling Beckwirth had fashioned for him. Taylor patted the earth flat with his shovel. He asked *Charro*, 'You want to say something?'

Charro nodded. He'd been a good Catholic boy once; he remembered the words to an old prayer. Listening, Taylor remembered the body in the corral, he thought how random and senseless death seemed; he was conscious of the vastness of this lonely plain, how insignificant one person was, measured against the desert and the mountains and the sky. He was conscious of his own mortality.

He supposed the others were thinking the same things. Gazing off to the north-east he told Beckwirth 'Someone's coming.'

'I don't see nothin'.'

'Horsebacker coming.'

A few minutes later, Beckwirth said, 'You're right. You got good eyes, Taylor.' After another minute studying the approaching rider, he declared, 'That might be Pete Olsen.'

'Olsen?'

'Sure. Grant County lawman. Ain't you heard of him? He's famous for—'

Taylor smiled wryly. 'I know what he's famous for.'

Olsen was riding a bayo coyote, a dun horse with a black stripe along the spine. Eyeing the horse, Taylor made a sound of admiration in his throat. Olsen reined in his mount. He studied the new grave and the three men standing by it. He asked, 'Dan Beckwirth, ain't it?'

'Olsen.'

Pete Olsen was a stocky man, with a square, wide-mouthed face. Sometime in the past Olsen's nose had been broken; perhaps at the same time, perhaps on another occasion, he'd obtained a long scar on his right cheek, a deep wound shaped something like a question mark. The scar, the broken nose, the splayed teeth, gave his face, which wasn't handsome to begin with, a startling, almost malevolent ugliness. He didn't attempt to soften his appearance with either moustache or beard. Nor was he fair-skinned as his Norwegian or Swedish name might indicate; the hair that fell to his shoulders in greasy rats' tails was mud-coloured.

Beckwirth said, 'This is Calvin Taylor.'

Olsen lifted a hand and rubbed the stubble on his scarred cheek. 'Well, well. I've heard of you.' His voice was cracked with dust and thirst and knowing the mountain trail down from Grant County, Taylor could sympathize. Frontier etiquette required that the newcomer stayed in the saddle until invited to dismount. Taylor said, 'Step down.'

Olsen swung out of the saddle. He asked, 'Who's dead?'

Beckwirth said, 'Horsethieves tried for the stock this morning. One of 'em got shot doing it.'

'Sweet Jesus. Who done the man-killing?'

'Taylor here. He wounded that one.' Beckwirth nodded towards *Charro*

Olsen grinned. 'I hear tell you've put under more men than the typhus, Taylor.'

Beckwirth said, 'That ain't all. He shot one of them horses in the corral gateway, sort of stoppered up the gate. Saved the company stock.'

Taylor shifted uncomfortably. He felt embarrassed, these men talking about him as if he wasn't even there.

Olsen said, 'Shot two thieves and saved the horses. All in a morning's work, eh Taylor? They hear about this in Tucson, they'll likely elect you governor.'

Taylor said, 'Hope not.'

Olsen patted his saddle. 'I got a jug of Mex liquor here. Pulque. Anybody care to join me?'

Beckwirth said, 'I could fix something to eat, first.'

Olsen mopped the last slick of bacon grease from his tin plate with a sourdough biscuit. He swallowed a soda sinker smeared with molasses, drank half a cupful of Arbuckle coffee and belched ripely. In Mexico and the border country a belch of such proportions was a compliment for good cooking. He told Beckwirth, 'From what I hear, you cook a sight better than you shoot!' Sweat darkened the armpits of his flannel shirt. The inside of the waystation was muggy with heat.

Taylor washed his face in a tin bowl, considering his reflection in a fragment of mirror as he did so. He had a dark face, almost dark enough for an Indian; but his features had nothing Indian about them. His hair was dark brown, not the blue-black of Indian hair. He fingered one end of his moustache. He was thirty years old, but looked older, he decided. He was starting to look tired before his time.

Olsen's voice brought Taylor back from his thoughts. Olsen asked, 'What do you figger to do with that greaser?'

Taylor dried his hands. 'Greaser?'

'That horsethief?'

'Take him back to Tucson.'

Tucson was perhaps fifty miles to the north and west. Olsen asked, 'Why?'

'People I work for there.'

'I hear you got hired by some of the big ranch owners down here. Pete Kitchen, John Slaughter, the likes of them. Or do they still kill their own snakes?'

Taylor picked a sliver of bacon from between his teeth. 'I heard you was a Grant County lawman. You're out of your patch.'

'I been hired to run down who's organizing all this stock thieving. I don't care which damn county I'm in.'

'What makes you think it's being organized? There's always been stock thieving in this country.'

Olsen drunk from the pulque jug, belched and wiped his mouth with the back of his wrist. 'Not as bad as it's been this year. You hear about the Doc Middleton band? Horsethieves up in Nebraska? Took the army, General Crook hisself, to run them down. Well, there's something like that been set up around here, and somebody leads 'em. That's what those … people you work for think too, ain't it? That's why they got together and hired the great Calvin Taylor. The great range detective.'

Taylor smiled grudgingly. 'Supposin' you're right....'

'Well?'

'If it is organized, there's a whole band of them, they need a hideout, for them and what they steal. It'll have to have water and grass. The rains are late this spring, the flatlands are dry. So that means somewhere in the high country. Some canyon maybe, up in the mountains. Perfect place'd be a canyon that gets wide in the middle, spreads out to meadows.'

Beckwirth said, 'What they'd call a "hole" up north.'

Olsen fingered the scar on his cheek. ''Course, something like that could be across the border in Mexico, couldn't it?'

Taylor nodded.

Olsen asked, 'When you taking your prisoner to Tucson, Taylor?'

'Tomorrow.'

'All right if I ride along? Two can stand guard better than one.'

Taylor shrugged.

Olsen drank again. 'So you figger we're looking for a robbers' roost?'

Taylor grunted a yes. 'We find that hideout, we can break this rustlers' thing.'

'If it's this side of the border.'

'If it is or if it ain't.'

'You don't even care what *country* you're in, huh?' Olsen grinned. 'You're a man after my own heart, Taylor.'

TWO

At dusk the following day, the riders halted in the desert.

Taylor rode a lineback horse, a dun with a black stripe along its spine. The *charro* rode a grey pony, judged the cheapest animal in the Coyote Springs saddleband. Olsen rode his fine coyote horse. They hadn't pushed their animals through the day's heat and were still about twenty miles from Tucson.

This remained dangerous country. The Indian Wars were officially over; most of the Apache bands were corraled on reservations. Even the terrible Chiricahuas were turning into good Indians, dirt-farming on the San Carlos Agency. But the peace was new, no one trusted it yet. There were still a few renegade Chiricahua and Mexican Apache bands hiding out in the Sierra Madre, across the border in Mexico. It was also a country of horsethieves, Indian, Mexican and Anglo. So Olsen, picketing the horses, and Taylor, who drew the cooking duties, both kept their rifles close to hand.

After eating a meal of prairie chicken – which, in the cactus and cattle country, almost never meant chicken and almost always meant bacon and beans – the travellers had a dessert of sweet, purple-red fruit. Taylor cut slices of this from a prickly pear. Olsen guessed this was something Taylor had learned about from the Indians, not the only thing he'd learned, if rumour was to be believed....

Olsen watched Taylor eating. He supposed women might think the range detective was a handsome man; they might like the mixing of dark complexion and blue eyes and dark hair. Olsen's thoughts always became bitter when it came to women. He had to pay for his. But they were all whores; they all wanted paying in one way or another.

Olsen poured coffee into a tin cup. He shaped a cornshuck cigarette. He glanced over at *Charro*, sitting near the horses, his hands tied before him. Olsen had started to object when Taylor fed the prisoner bacon too, but he'd let it go. He'd pick his time.

The sunset was dull copper behind the mountains, above the black land. Giant saguaro were like weird, mutilated hands clutching convulsively at the sky. Olsen heard dusk sounds, red-spotted toads croaking, the hooing of a horned owl. He heard the regular chewing noises the horses made, eating beans off the mesquite trees.

Taylor seemed to have the typical cowman's aversion to words, so Olsen talked, filling in the silence between them. He said, 'Them horsethieves – they could be operating out of Cochise County. We run the Earp gang out of the country, but that's still a goddam sin pit. Still lousy with horsethieves.' Olsen spat. 'What you figger?'

The range detective didn't reply.

'You sure talk the ass end off a muley cow, Taylor!' Olsen declared, grinning. 'How come you talk so goddam much?'

Taylor turned the tin cup in his hand. 'Just can't shut my mouth I guess.'

Olsen formed another cigarette. "Course, there could be reds in this too. I believe Apaches is peaceful when the whole root and branch is cleaned out! Thievingest, lousiest, stinkingest bastards on God's earth.' He licked his cigarette papers, glancing quickly at the other man to see how his words were going down. 'I say kill the lot of them.' He lit the cigarette and spent a moment studying the thin lines of smoke that trailed from his nostrils. Then he looked at Taylor. He said, 'I've heard a lot about you.'

'Oh?'

'A few years back you was scouting against the Apaches. Victorio, Nana, real bad ones. I hear them *broncos* used to scare their kids, tellin' 'em if they weren't good little Indians, you'd come and get them. What them Indians call you? Shadow Man, something like that. What's that mean?'

'Hard to explain. A shadow ain't just a shadow to an Indian.'

Olsen smoked a moment. He said, 'Next I hear, you're hiring out to all the big ranchers. They're calling you a "stock detective" or a "range detective". What's that mean, you catch any stock thieves you can pull the trigger on 'em legal? Just how legal are you, Taylor?'

Taylor didn't reply.

Olsen drank coffee. 'The lone wolf they call you. Badman's bad luck! The undertaker's joy! A man had you on his heels, he'd better just turn hisself in, then and there, or cut his own throat, or he'd end up off in the lonelies somewhere, under the buzzards. So I heard.'

In a bored voice, Taylor advised, 'Don't believe everything you hear.'

'You sure are a disappointment to me.'

Taylor smiled faintly. 'I am?'

The lawman smiled a thin smile also. 'I had you figgered for the all-time, ice-cold, professional mankiller. The real McCoy. But I think you're soft, Taylor. Take that horsethief.' He nodded towards the Mexican. 'We got to drag that greaser all the way to Tucson. Why? There's only one thing you do with horsetheives. Only difference is how you do it. You know about "the death of the skins"? Wrap someone in a wet steerhide and let it shrink on them. Or get a knife and heat the blade. Then this peppergut might tell us something; where them robbers have their roost; who heads 'em up. And if he doesn't talk … who cares? One horsethief less. But seems you ain't got the guts for that kind of business.'

The lawman lifted his tin cup to his lips. He glimpsed, to his surprise, reaction in Taylor's face; he was sure he caught, fleetingly, what might be a look of uncertainty in the other man's eyes. Olsen had only been trying to needle Taylor, but it had worked! Taylor was starting to have some doubts about himself!

Having found one nerve, Olsen probed for another. 'Still think there might be Indians tied up in this too. Them red niggers up on the reservation. What you figger? I hear tell you're the *real* Indian expert.'

Taylor placed his coffee cup carefully on the earth before him. He stared at the other man. 'You could make that plainer, Olsen.'

The lawman grinned. 'Sleep time. I'll take first watch.'

Olsen's first watch, of three hours, passed without incident, as did Taylor's. Olsen's second stint on guard took him to the beginnings of false dawn. It was at that time that the prisoner must have got his hands free. Olsen discovered this when a very hard object struck him at the base of the skull, just behind the right ear. The next thing he discovered was that full light had come, he was lying face down on the sand. His head roared with pain. He sat up and threw up last night's supper over his legs and the bottom of his shirt. After a time he got to his feet, one hand pressing down the pain in the side of his head. He looked at the blood on his fingers and swore.

The first thing Olsen looked for when his head cleared was the coyote horse. It wasn't there. Olsen felt anger, so much anger he almost forgot his headache. The prisoner was gone, as were the horses.

And so was Calvin Taylor.

THREE

Ten days later, Augustin Jarocha reached the Canyon of The Dead.

He dismounted from the bayo coyote and spent a few minutes examining the horse's ankles and feet. It hurt him to see how hard travel through rough country had worn the animal down. He'd let the other horse, Calvin Taylor's lineback, go yesterday; riding change and change about had spared both animals, but he guessed the lineback had no more run in him and would die within the first mile of any resumed journey.

If there was any softness left in Jarocha, he supposed it was for horses. He'd found real pleasure in his recent work, which was acquiring horses without benefit of a bill of sale. For a few days they were his, he could imagine he was a *rico*, a nobleman or a rich man's son, with his pick of the best riding stock; or at least a top cowhand, a real *charro*, which he'd once almost been.

The coyote horse was gaunt now, but a few days' rest on the good grass and feed of the canyon, would bring it back into condition. He was almost tempted to try and keep it; but he knew it would be the price charged for entry back into the canyon. The horse would buy him a place to rest up for a few days, a secure place which is what you needed with the likes of Calvin Taylor and 'Swede' Olsen on your trail ... and perhaps not just them....

Ten miles north, he'd almost ridden into a patrol of *rurales*, state policemen. They rarely came so deep into the back country, and Jarocha wondered if they were here looking for the robbers' roost, but that seemed doubtful. For one thing, there were only a dozen of them, and it would need a small army to take on the roost; for another, the *rurales* wouldn't care about thieves who only stole north of the border, raiding the *gringos*; they would probably give the robbers their unofficial blessing.

For all that, *rurales* had a sinister reputation. They were a tough crew. They had to be; a handful of policemen trying to enforce law and order in the vastness of northern Mexico, a wilderness of bandits, smugglers and wild Indians. It was curious, for instance, how many prisoners taken by *rurales* never made it to trial; instead they got themselves killed 'trying to escape'. It was called the law of *ley fuga*. A suspicious-looking vagrant, especially on a horse like the bayo coyote, could anticipate similar treatment. So Jarocha waited in cover, watching the *rurales* file past, men in leather chaps and wide sombreros, rifles in their saddle scabbards, chests crossed with cartridge belts, and waited until their grey jackets had dimmed into distance. He was glad to see they were riding north; Jarocha had headed south.

His journey had punished him as well as the horse. He rubbed at his aching back, then sat on the earth, kneading the cramps out of his thighs and legs. He was bone-tired; he glanced at his battered *charro* clothing, scraping the tips of his fingers against the dust on his cheek, feeling the stubble on his chin. Once he'd been a man who liked to dress well, to stay clean. He felt disgust for himself, for almost everything he thought about; everything but the bayo coyote.

With the first darkness he got into his bedroll and closed his eyes. Tomorrow he'd have the company of others around him; not so much friends, he told himself, because he liked to think he was better than most of them, but more of his kind. There'd be food and drink, perhaps a woman ... that was something to think about. For a few days he'd be safe.

One thing still disturbed him: the two Anglo lawmen on his trail. Well, Olsen was official law, a deputy sheriff out of Grant County. Who could say what Taylor was officially ... but Jarocha was uneasy about them. Somehow, he'd escaped them too easily. It had been Taylor's fault; he hadn't tied the prisoner's hands securely enough, which seemed a very odd mistake to make. As Taylor and Olsen sat around the campfire, talking, Jarocha had thought about that; he thought about it later, lying in his bedroll, while Olsen and then Taylor took the watch. Were they setting him up, were the Anglos trying a little *ley fuga* of their own, an excuse to rub out another greaser? But he'd decided to risk it. Olsen looked like he'd half-dozed off on his second watch; Jarocha worked his hands free; there'd been a limb of mesquite lying nearby, just about perfect as a club ... strange that was there ... and he'd used the club on Olsen. *That* was the really strange part, no matter how quiet you were, you could scarcely strike anyone on the head with a spar of hardwood without making a noise that ought to have brought Taylor from his bedroll. Back at Coyote Springs, his hearing had been sharp enough ... but the man never stirred. Only when Jarocha was dusting out of camp, on Olsen's horse, leading the lineback dun, did he glimpse Taylor moving, sitting up....

It didn't make sense, Taylor being so slow and careless. Had he let Jerocha escape deliberately, in order to trail him here?

Because he'd thought that, Jarocha had set up a false trail, first going east, towards Cochise County, before zigzagging south and west, crossing the border from the Papago Reservation and heading south into the Mexican mountains. After two days he was convinced he'd outdistanced any pursuit, there was no one on his trail. And yet....

Jarocha opened his eyes studying the brooding canyon darkness. The Canyon of The Dead. Perhaps it was this place that was spooking him, the legends about it; or perhaps it was those *rurales* today. He made a sound of disgust. He closed his eyes and pulled the blanket up under his chin. Forget Taylor, the white Indian, Olsen, the ugly man with his splayed teeth and scarred cheek, the ghosts of Dead Canyon ... there'd be whiskey tomorrow, and a bath, and cards, maybe a woman.

Something like a metal thumb, cold and very hard, was pressing into the back of his head, just behind the right ear. Jarocha blinked himself awake. Dawn, pink light on the canyon roof, leaking down the canyon sides. The lower canyon grey, paling as he looked. Cold metal behind his right ear. Fear suddenly jumped in him, he started in his bed, as if he'd fallen in a dream; he saw a dim shape, darker than the gloom of the canyon floor, hunched over him. The shape held a rifle, the end of the barrel resting against the base of Jarocha's skull.

The Mexican swore.

Calvin Taylor said, 'Morning.'

Jarocha was told various things; to show his hands slowly, to lie on his face. He obeyed clumsily.

Taylor observed, 'You ain't at your best in the mornings, eh?'

'Some mornings are better than others. You going to kill me?'

'No.'

'Then maybe this is my lucky morning.'

'Don't bet on it.' Taylor crouched down and Jarocha felt his hands being tied behind him. This time Taylor did the job properly. He stood. 'I'm going to hand you over to a *rurales* patrol that ain't too far off.'

Jarocha twisted over, got to his knees. 'The *rurales*? You're crazy.'

'Oh?'

'You're a Yankee lawman down here in Mexico. You've got no right to be here. They're more likely to shoot you than me, *gringo*.'

'Ordinarily, that might be true, though I don't think you can rightly call me a Yankee. But I know some of these particular *rurales*, and they know why I'm here. The captain and I once did a little cross-the-border ...' – he smiled faintly – 'trading, you might say.'

'You mean smuggling?'

'Also I was acquainted with his sister.'

Jarocha stood. 'If you hand me over to the *rurales* ... you know what they do. *Ley fuga*.' He heard the pleading tone in his voice.

The other man nodded slowly. 'But there's a little matter of some horses you stole. Including mine. Anyway, you said it yourself, *hombre*.'

Jarocha blinked at the look in Taylor's eyes; they were as hard as the eyes of an Indian, without pity or feeling. Jarocha swallowed; suddenly his stomach was cold with fear. 'Said what?'

Taylor's smile faded. 'Better a bullet than a rope.'

Taylor had said, 'Perfect place would be a canyon that gets wide in the middle, spreads out to meadows'. Something like that. Beckwirth had said 'What they'd call a "hole", up north'.

Taylor lifted the army field glasses to his eyes and studied one such perfect place.

He was on the roof of Dead Canyon. He studied the canyon floor several hundred feet below. Here was the 'hole', meadows of yellow grama grass, cupped by sheer granite walls. The basin was speckled with slow-moving shapes – several hundred horses, a few herds of cattle. In the lee of the orange cliffs was a cluster of dwellings – adobes, huts, tents. A few dug-outs pitted the cliff base. There were corrals too, for the stock, but the hole itself was a natural corral.

Taylor eased back from the edge of the canyon roof. He'd ground-hitched his two horses – the grey and Olsen's bayo coyote – in a nearby grove of juniper and piñon trees. He entered this grove.

He'd done his job, locating the robbers' roost. He'd leave the rest, cleaning out the roost, to the men who'd hired him, ranchers in Arizona. They'd need to act in considerable force; there might be fifty or a hundred men hiding in the canyon.

Taylor doubted they would get much help from the Mexican authorities; there was still a lot of ill-feeling between the two nations. His employers might be able to persuade the US Army to swoop down here, perhaps under the pretext of chasing bronco Indians across the border. Most likely, though, the ranchers would do the job themselves; get together a private army and raid across the line. But whatever they did, it was out of his hands. His principal concern now was getting out of this canyon with a whole skin.

A clever touch, locating here, in Cañón De La Muerte, the Canyon Of The Dead. According to an old story, there'd been a ranch here once. Perhaps the ranchers thought they were too far west for Apaches. But thirty or forty years ago, the Chiricahuas had raided through anyway, slaughtering everybody and burning the buildings. Now, in the deepest part of the night, the ghosts of the slain were said to walk the canyon, their screams torturing the darkness. The more superstitious believed these stories, and also the local Indians; they gave the canyon a wide berth. A more prosaic version of events was that the Apaches had found the ranch deserted and had to be content with just putting the buildings to the torch; but a good legend demanded the earth soaked with blood and the ground seeded with bones.

Taylor came from his thoughts. He saw the ears of the horses pointing to the east and he looked that way. He made out a dim shape standing in a clump of junipers, behind a screen of foliage; a green shadow that might be a man with a rifle in his hands.

The thing to do, Taylor decided, was not to show

he'd seen the man, but to keep walking over to his horse, then take action. Behind him he heard the click of a weapon coming on full cock.

He halted. He kept his hands well clear of his sides, and the pistol, butt forward in the holster on his left hip. He waited. He heard small noises, coming nearer; he decided there were two men behind him, approaching. The third man emerged from the shade of the junipers.

The men behind him halted. The other man walked over to the horses. He wore the uniform of a corporal in the US Cavalry, his army blouse crossed by a heavy, buckled shoulderstrap. Yellow facing piped his battered canvas pants. A black campaign hat shadowed his narrow face; he was thin, gangling. He carried a 45-70 Springfield 'Long Tom' rifle.

Taylor glanced at the two men behind him. One was nondescript, dressed like a miner, the other might be a Mexican cowboy. Both held rifles.

The corporal said, 'Get rid of the gun.' His accent made him a Texan. He had the Springfield trained on Taylor's stomach.

With his left hand, Taylor took a corner of the grip on his pistol. Very slowly, he lifted the weapon from the holster and threw it on to the earth.

The corporal nodded. This might have been a signal to each of his companions, as, simultaneously, all three men began to walk towards their new prisoner.

FOUR

Faces.

They swam before him. Some were bright as sunspots, too bright to look at; others were dim orbs; others came suddenly into sharp focus, hard-edged and angular. One face in particular. An Apache. It wasn't Nah-Lin; he might have expected to see her. This was a man with a friendly moon face, two eyes like black shoe buttons cut deep in his very dark bronze flesh. He had clubbed blue-black hair that fell to his chest, bound at the temples with a red sweat rag. The marks of smallpox pitted his right cheek. Taylor knew him, but from where? While he was thinking about that the face softened, melted into brightness and after a time shaped into the face of another man.

A man? Was it a man? Or even anything human? Or was it a block of stone, wide across the shoulders, stomach and jaw, the head a carved projection that grew from the thick trunk without benefit of neck, a red granite statue with an eagles beak and black, bottomless eyes; not a face but a death mask, like those the Anasazi, the Old Ones, cupped around the faces of their dead. Taylor wondered why this statue was upside down. Why were all the faces upside down?

Sometime later he remembered that they weren't; he was. He was tied to a wagon wheel, head pointing towards the earth. Flies covered him, he felt their tiny legs moving on his lips and eyelids. His vision was bleary, the images before him trembled and wandered left and right, with a brightness behind them painful to gaze into. The sounds he heard were thick and distorted, and then he heard a voice say, clearly, 'Cut the sonofabitch down.'

His limbs were freed. Limply, Taylor rolled on to his face.

A little later he tried to sit up. Someone threw a bucket of water in his face. The shock of it made him gasp. He blinked. The shape of the man standing over him, with the bucket, slowly became defined, became a corporal in the US Cavalry. The thin, gangling man with the Texan accent. Behind the soldier other men were standing; behind them were tents, huts and adobes; behind them the cliff face. He remembered where he was now, he was a prisoner in the roost, the robbers' hideout in Dead Canyon.

Another man stood at the corporal's side, then slowly lowered himself to earth, wedging himself in the angle between two adobe walls. This was the man with the massive square face, the red statue. He had a hook nose, a black beard that curled to his chest, bull-like shoulders and neck. The man became a dim, wavering shape again; Taylor felt pain like a slow, dull hammer in his head, sharp pain like fishhooks in his eyes. He vomited. Someone threw water on his head and shoulders, he heard the voice say, 'Let him drink.' There was a canteen against his lips, water running into his mouth and throat.

After a time, his vision cleared once more. He saw the corporal and other men standing about, Anglos and Mexicans, all sporting weapons of various kinds – rifles, pistols, knives, and hung with ammunition belts. He glanced at the man sitting in the shade of the adobe walls, not on the earth as Taylor had first thought, but perching his bulk on a footstool. This man said, 'My name is Zachary Powers. You could say I run things around here. Who are you, sir?'

Taylor drank again. Powers smiled patiently. He produced a grubby handkerchief and mopped his red face. He was sweating badly, which wasn't surprising given that the man was wearing a black broadcloth suit. He would stand, Taylor guessed, a head above six feet, his arms and shoulders showed the man he once was, the tumbling stomach the man he'd become.

Taylor said, 'Name's Dave Brewer. I got into some shooting trouble up in the Santa Ritas. Over someone else's horse. That's what I tried to tell your friend there.' Taylor nodded towards the corporal.

Powers gazed at the soldier. 'Well, Griffin?'

Griffin sneered. 'I didn't believe that bullshit.'

Powers took a slender briar pipe from his waistcoat pocket and carefully wadded shag into the bowl. 'And why don't you believe him? Did he bring the horses with him?'

Griffin said, 'Two good horses.'

'Then I see no reason to disbelieve him.' Powers smiled. He asked Taylor, 'You will dine with me, sir?'

Powers and Taylor entered the adobe. Someone kept the dwelling clean; Indian rugs covered the floor or were draped on the walls. There was even a tablecloth over the long plank table in the centre of the room. Clay bowls of water hung from the low ceiling, to help the room cool.

Both men sat at the table. Powers produced a Remington-Rider pocket revolver and laid it on the table before him. He discarded his broadcloth coat, vest and stringtie, then donned a grimy bib. A Mexican woman brought them food – chilis, tamales, tortillas and a bottle of Baconora Mescal. She left.

Was he strong and quick enough, Taylor thought, to reach the mescal bottle and kill Powers with it, before the other man used the pocket revolver? Could he spill the table on to Powers and pin him under it? Cut off the snake's head and the snake dies ... and Powers was the head of this particular nest of snakes. But was he the sole leader, or were there others in this too?

Taylor judged the table was too heavy to upend, especially as he still felt weak from his time spread against the wheel. Powers' bulk would make him slow, but he could still grab the pistol before Taylor reached him. Not that Taylor was thinking about it seriously. He guessed there was a guard sitting outside the door of the adobe, even now ... so Taylor attended to the meal, picking slowly at the food.

Powers ate furiously. Taylor was impressed by the quantity the man ate and the speed of his eating. When he'd finished, Powers slumped back in his chair, belched ripely, unhinged his bib and used it to wipe his mouth. He poured himself two fingers of mescal. His already florid face was brick-red, sweat ran from him. He drank and spent the next few minutes coughing into his fist. He declared, 'Goddam Mex liquor!' He poured mescal into another toothglass and pushed the glass across the table towards the other man.

Powers said, 'Settling for second-best drinking whiskey is one disadvantage – perhaps the main disadvantage – of living out here in the wilderness. You agree, Brewer? Here we are, with nothing in any direction for fifty or a hundred miles. Not even the local Indians come around here. Too superstitious. We are surrounded by a moat of desolation, legend, fear. Water all year round. Graze. Just about perfect for our needs.

Taylor drank mescal. 'Just about.'

'This canyon wasn't left empty long after the Apaches burned the old ranch. Smugglers used it. Then army deserters built a roost here. Now, as you see, other types of humanity are drawn here. Men cast out of conventional society because they refuse to be governed by the ridiculous mores that shackle that society. Men like you and I, Mr Brewer. Outlawed by our own enterprise, daring. Left here in these mountains. Appropriately enough.' He smiled. 'The Ladrones – the "Robber Mountains". I control this canyon. I decide who enters ... who stays ... who leaves. I give them protection, in return for a share of what they take. And men without the benefit of my protection ...' – he studied his toothglass, his lips twisting mirthlessly – 'don't survive.'

Taylor took his Bible papers – his cigarette papers – from his tobacco pouch and shaped a cigarette.

Powers said, 'This place is not just a refuge to me, Brewer, it's a beginning. I intend – and soon – to descend like Moses. Armed not with tablets of stone, but more. Respectability! Why not? What's respectability after all but money … success? I shall emerge from this exile a man of wealth and property.'

Powers coughed again. He turned his head and spat on to the Navaho carpet on the floor behind him. He said, 'Goddam!' Taylor heard another man cough, on the other side of the adobe door; the guard that Taylor had expected to be there.

Powers poured another drink for himself. 'Look at all the big, respectable ranch owners in Arizona. All of 'em got started on stolen Mexican beef and horses! No, Mr Brewer, my interests are not solely the profit margins of a robber's roost. Already I have made important contacts. Both sides of the border. The Mexican army is mounting a big campaign to wipe out the Yaqui Indians. They want beef and horses and they don't give a damn where it comes from. But I have buyers on the American side of the line, too.' Powers lifted his head, he scratched his beard and the underside of his chin. He said, 'Choddi!'

The man in the doorway coughed again, opened the steerhide door and stepped into the room.

Taylor stared.

The newcomer was an Apache. He wore moccasins that reached over his knees, a filthy smock and cut-away pants, a white-man's brocaded waistcoat. His long hair was tied with a red sweat rag. He carried a Henry carbine in one hand and, in the other, a nearly empty bottle. He grinned foolishly and Taylor smelt whiskey on his breath. Taylor felt his stomach tighten in fear. Any white-eye might be frightened of a drunken Apache with a modern weapon in his hands; but

Taylor was frightened for other reasons. He's seen this man before; he remembered the easy grin and the pock-marked right cheek.

The Indian belched and giggled. He grinned at Taylor again. In Apache he said, 'Hello, Shadow Man.'

Powers lifted the pocket gun with his right hand and pointed the weapon at Taylor's chest. He said, 'Please finish you whiskey, Mr Taylor.'

The Apache swayed slightly. He asked Powers, 'You want me to shoot him now?'

'Maybe you'll get to shoot him later, Choddi.'

Choddi – his name meant Antelope – shrugged. He asked Taylor, 'Hey, Shadow Man, you remember when we chased Victorio's men from Rattlesnake Springs?' He didn't wait for a reply but sat on the floor, the rifle across his knees and drank noisily from the bottle.

Powers laid the revolver on the table beside him. He said, 'You are Calvin Taylor, the celebrated range detective. Choddi, of course, knew you back in the days when he was a "good" Indian. I knew who you were from the start.'

Taylor drank mescal. 'But you didn't say.'

'Permit me some small form of amusement, Mr Taylor. This deception amused me. And you can't appreciate how much I miss an intelligent conversation with an educated man.'

'Ain't you still missing it?'

Powers chuckled. 'You're clearly a self-educated man, sir. Someone tutored by wide experience. You have a considerable reputation in your field.'

'Do any good to tell you: sure, I got hired to catch horsethieves, but since then I've had a falling out with a Grant County lawman, now I'm on the dodge too.'

The other man smiled tiredly. 'It's regrettable we can't work together, Mr Taylor. A wealth of possibilities. But I suspect your loyalty would ever be in doubt.'

Choddi pushed himself slowly to his feet.

Powers said, 'Now I'll bid you goodnight, Mr Taylor. Choddi will see you to your bed. A little adobe we use for the purpose of incarceration.' He lifted the pistol again and pointed it at the range detective. 'We seem to be short of one piece of cultery, so if you stand quite still Choddi will remove the knife from down the side of your boot. So you don't cut yourself.' He lifted the crumpled bib, wiping it once again across his mouth. 'I could, I suppose, offer you a soft death. But I wouldn't wish to insult you.'

'I can stand a few insults.'

Another ironic smile. Powers said, 'In this case I'm sure you can. But you should appreciate the principle involved having spent time amongst the wild savages. Amongst the Indian tribes, I believe, punishment and torture are directly proportionate to the courage and worth of the victim. The braver the victim, the harder the death. Is that not correct? I often think we can learn a good deal more from the savages than many credit. So I must offer you a death equal to your reputation. A hard death. A kind of flattery, in a way. But you must have expected the same when you were captured.'

'Sure.' Taylor said. 'I appreciate it.'

FIVE

Next morning, two men came and took Taylor from the hut where he'd been held prisoner. One of these men was the Texan, Griffin, lately a corporal in the Sixth Cavalry, until he'd deserted his enlistment. The other was Cullen Anders. He was a thin boy not yet out of his teens. He had sandy hair and the pale beginnings of a moustache. He dressed like a cowboy, a pleasant enough looking youth except for his eyes. There was a wild cast to them; nobody would have trusted him because of his eyes. There was a nervousness in the boy that made Taylor doubly uneasy and fear was already a cold rottenness twisting in his belly.

The two men could have put a bullet in Taylor then and there but they were about a more complicated game and seemed determined to enjoy themselves. Lots of smirking and knowing grins passed between them. Taylor was imagining what form Powers 'hard death' might take, but he wasn't going to ask; he knew his captors would tell him eventually.

Anders led up three horses, Taylor was told to mount a paint horse. His hands were tied to the pommel of the saddle. The two others mounted their horses and Anders rode off leading Taylor's

paint by a rope around its neck. Grffin brought up
the rear. The three riders rode in file along the
canyon until they came to a place where a
zigzagging trail gouged the canyon wall, climbing
to the canyon roof. The three men ascended this
trail, sometimes dismounting where the slope was
too steep. They made slow going, in the eye of the
sun. Once on the canyon roof, they found a small
bosky of piñon and jojoba trees and sat in the
shade. Anders made some coffee. Griffin said,
'Let's be decent. Make sure Taylor has some too.'
He grinned.

Anders grinned also. He said, 'Sure.'

As Taylor drank, Griffin observed, 'That's your
last cup of coffee, Taylor.'

Anders chuckled. He kept putting his hand on
the knife at his belt. It was a Bowie knife, pretty
much an antique these days but still a fearsome
weapon. The knife, with its twelve-inch blade,
seemed almost obscenely large on the thigh of the
boy. Of all weapons, Taylor had always hated the
Bowie knife. He wondered what kind of man Jim
Bowie must have been: from all accounts he was at
home in polite society, amongst the business world
of the Deep South and old Mexico, yet there was
the other Bowie, who killed men with a huge,
one-pound, butcher's knife that ended in a wicked,
double-edged point.

Anders said, 'What you got in mind for this
feller, Griffin?'

'I thought maybe....' Griffin scratched the
underside of his chin.

'Yeah?'

'Ants!'

Anders laughed out loud. It was a shrill, not

quite sane laugh; Taylor had already decided the boy wasn't quite right in the head. 'Ants?'

'Sure. Stake him out on an anthill. I got some sorghum in one of my canteens, we can pour that all over him and watch them ants go to work.'

'I don't think I can do that to a white man.'

Griffin snorted. 'Skin colour is white, but that don't make him a white man! He's run with the Apaches. Lived with 'em, squawed with 'em, prefers them to his own people!' The Texan spat. 'Ain't nothing lower on earth than a white man breeds with red bitches. Or a white man runs with Indians.'

Anders nodded. 'How about cutting off his eyelids, so he can get a good look at the sun? That's real Apache, ain't it? Just right for the likes of him.' He took the Bowie knife from the sheath and tested the edge of the blade against his fingers.

Griffin said, 'You're learning fast, kid.'

Taylor remembered a canyon off the west side of the Peloncillo Mountains – Skeleton Canyon? – and something the Apaches he was trailing had left behind, to mark their passing. They'd buried the man up to his neck in the middle of an anthill, black and red with harvester ants, and covered his head with cactus juice. It was the only time Taylor had seen that done; the ants had been thorough....

Coffee finished, they mounted their horses and rode northward into rougher country. They came to broken ground where the land sloped away, in some places steeply, towards the desert floor. Taylor supposed his captors must have their minds set on one particular anthill to go to all this trouble.

Griffin said, 'Hold up.'

The riders halted at the top of a sharp, rubbled

decline that pitched down into a tangle of shoulder-high chaparral and saguaro. The Texan said, 'We lead the horses down here. Cullen, see to him.'

The boy grinned, dismounted and walked over to Taylor. The Texan kept his Springfield pointing at the prisoner. Anders kept one hand on the grip of the Colt pistol worn backwards on his left hip. He lifted the rope from the paint's head and tossed the noosed end over Taylor's head, so that the rope settled on the prisoner's shoulders; Anders threw the other end of the rope to Griffin. The Texan gave the rope an experimental tug. Taylor jerked, swayed and almost fell from the saddle; he felt the noose burn into his neck. Griffin laughed. Anders giggled and pulled the Bowie from its sheath. He stood a moment, grinning, the terrible weapon in his fist. Then he stepped forward and began to cut the rope that fastened Taylor's wrists to the saddle horn.

Taylor decided that his captors had made two mistakes: one was that Anders was now in between Griffin and the prisoner, in the Texan's line of fire. Griffin must have realized this for he jumped his horse sideways.

The rope around Taylor's wrists parted.

Griffin began to step back; Taylor grabbed downwards, seizing both of Anders' wrists. He pitched from the saddle. Falling, he pulled Anders to his knees hooking one knee hard into the boy's groin. The horse behind him whinnied and shied away. He glimpsed Griffin turning his horse in a smother of dust. But there was no room for the Texan to go backwards or sideways up this trail; this was the second mistake he'd made. He couldn't find room to yank on the rope, to pull the prisoner clear of Anders. He dropped the rope instead and lifted the Springfield.

Anders and Taylor strained together. The boy was trying to lift the knife, his face reddening with effort; he was also trying to reach the grip of his pistol. Taylor used all his strength to force the other's hands down, to turn the knife into Anders' stomach. He was the stronger man; he was succeeding.

Griffin yelled, 'Get clear, Cullen!'

Anders tried to pull back, his arms, his whole body, quivering, his face dark with heat, but he couldn't break Taylor's grip. Griffin called, 'Get clear, or I'll have to shoot you both!'

Anders lifted his head and gave a cry of frustrated rage. Griffin's rifle cracked; Anders was knocked forward, slammed against Taylor and both men went down. Taylor glimpsed Griffin jumping his horse forward. Taylor released his grip on Anders' right wrist and grabbed the handle of the Colt in the backwards holster. He lifted the weapon, cocked it and fired. The Texan's horse reared away. Anders was lolling against Taylor's chest, but he was dead weight; Taylor glimpsed blood all over the back of his shirt. Over the dead man's shoulder, he saw Griffin wheeling his horse about, lifting his rifle again. Taylor let Anders fall. He grabbed the Bowie knife, turned sideways and sprang from the slope. He hit a dozen yards lower, on his left hip, numbing his leg, and rolled, in dust and loose stones, into a tangle of brush. He heard Griffin's rifle crack again; then he was ploughing into cover. Thorns raked him and he cried out. He banged his knuckles on a rock and lost his grip on the knife. He fetched up against the base of a saguaro, coughing on dust, feeling he'd broken every bone. He had no wind left, but he kept moving all the same, squirming behind the giant cactus, finding a boulder to lodge behind.

Griffin's rifle sounded once more, but the shot didn't come close. Taylor still had Anders' pistol in his hand and the fingers hinged around the grip ached. He lifted his head very slowly and gazed over the top of the boulder. He must have fallen or slithered a hundred yards downslope, out of effective pistol range, but Griffin hadn't come after him; he still sat his horse in the same place, Anders' body twisted on the earth nearby. The Texan suddenly jumped his horse sideways into cover and vanished from sight. After a minute, Taylor heard the sound of hooves going upslope, away from him.

Taylor waited, suspecting a trick; Griffin could have sent the horse upslope, riderless, and was creeping downslope afoot, after his enemy. But after ten minutes Taylor decided he hadn't done that. Perhaps he didn't care for a man-to-man game of hide-and-seek in deep cover, against a man who'd lived with the savage Apache, someone with Taylor's reputation. For which reputation, deserved or otherwise, Taylor duly gave thanks. Not that he was out of the woods. Griffin would undoubtedly return to the pursuit with more men and fresh horses; and Taylor was alone and almost defenceless in hostile country.

Taylor walked upslope. The horses had bolted, but Taylor took Anders' ammunition belt, with nineteen shells in the loops. He also took the length of rope his captors had used on him; then he moved downslope. He had, he calculated, fifty miles to cross to the safety of the Arizona line.

SIX

Griffin formed a posse. Four men – himself, the Apache Choddi, Dutch Charlie, Jubilee. They took fresh horses and set off northwards.

There were two courses open to Taylor, Griffin reasoned. The first was to put as much distance as possible before dark between himself and pursuit. The second was to lie up close by and waylay someone passing in or out of the roost. He needed three things fairly desperately – water, a horse and a rifle.

Griffin was right but Taylor was more daring – or perhaps more desperate – than the Texan realized. Whilst his pursuers rode northward, Taylor made his way back to the canyon roof. Sometime in the early part of the night one of the roost's residents was riding across the tableland above the canyon, a nearly empty bottle of *sotol* swinging in one hand. He had, afterwards, a vague memory of a whirring sound in the air above him, a rope falling over his head and pinning his arms to his sides. He remembered being jerked backwards … then it was dawn. He lay tied in the brush, his head pounding; he'd brought up last night's liquor over the front of his shirt. There was a Colt pistol lying in the dust nearby. He guessed he'd been struck on the head with the weapon, as the cedar-wood grip seemed to have broken off. His own pistol was gone, as was his rifle, canteen and his grey horse.

Calvin Taylor now had them; but his luck wasn't perfect. The horse he'd acquired from the horsethief had a stone bruise on its right forehoof.

Choddi squatted down, studying the earth below him.

Griffin said, 'Well?'

The Indian didn't reply. Indians were like that, Griffin knew; they took their own sweet time about doing anything and if you asked them a question they might chew it over for hours before saying anything. You couldn't hurry them as they seemed to have no idea that there was a finite limit to everyone's time. Griffin didn't like riding in the company of the Apache, even if he was a scout for the army once. However they needed him; he was their best tracker.

Jubilee took his canteen from his saddle and drank. He was a handsome young man, in shabby cowboy gear, a light-skinned Negro; he was light skinned because it was said his mother was a Choctaw Indian, his father a slave. He'd been a soldier too until he'd decamped from the Tenth Cavalry. Griffin didn't like riding with the Negro either, because he was black. Griffin despised anyone whose skin wasn't white.

Dutch Charlie asked, 'Well, is it Taylor?'

Choddi replied, 'Horse limping, right forehoof.'

Dutch Charlie snorted. A knife cut had ripped one side of his nose, paring away the right nostril and giving him a particularly expressive snort. The scar ran on, up across his forehead, into his carroty hair. Like his companions, Charlie had left the employ of the US Army unofficially. He was a 'snowbird', he'd come west with the army, lived one winter on army rations and deserted in the spring.

Griffin saw Charlie was gazing at him with distaste. Maybe he was thinking how Griffin had let the prisoner escape. The Texan felt a quick anger. He decided he despised Dutch Charlie too, and this time skin colour had nothing to do with it. He said, 'Has to be Taylor.'

Charlie asked, 'How do you know?' His voice was still heavy with a German accent.

'Who else'd be leading a half-lame horse into that rough country?' The Texan nodded towards the broken ground to the north.

Jubilee said, 'If he's took a horse off somebody, he could've got hold of a rifle too. He might lie up for us.'

Griffin shaped a cigarette. 'We'll send the Indian out ahead as scout, so Taylor doesn't jump us. Don't worry.' He showed his yellow teeth in the nearest approximation to a smile he could manage. 'We'll get that sonofabitch.'

Taylor swore.

He slipped from horseback and crouched down looking at the right forehoof of the grey horse. He made a face at what he saw, stood and took the canteen from the saddle. He drank briefly; in the same instant he saw movement, off to the south-west.

He'd halted in the cover of some mesquite and palo verde trees, just beyond a ridge. No one would

see him there, but he could see *them*. Three riders
in file, three flies crawling out of broken ground on
to the open plain, moving towards him. They
entered timber, dust riffled through a green belt of
scrub oak. His pursuers were driving their horses
too hard in the noontime heat. He'd hoped he'd
lost them, or that they'd given up. He must have
put twenty miles between himself and the roost
before the horse went lame; now it looked as if his
pursuers would follow him all the way to the
American line.

Unless he stopped them.

He swore again and touched the stock of the
Spencer carbine booted on the saddle of the horse.
How far away were they? How much time had he?
His eye was already hunting over broken ground,
looking for a place....

When the first shot came, Choddi halted his paint
pony. He dismounted, grabbed the horse's jawline
and backed the paint into the shadow of some
mesquite trees. The Apache's strong hands cupped
the horse's nostrils and throat. He had trained the
horse with gentleness and patience but he enforced
his mastery ruthlessly. The animal rolled its eyes,
shuffled its feet, shook it head. Choddi used his
sweatband to bind its nose.

The shot came from the north-east, perhaps
three miles distant, which meant Griffin and the
others had met up with Shadow Man, who'd got
around him somehow; or they'd run into someone
else, perhaps the *rurales* patrol that had been seen
around here a few days ago.

When someone made a gun smoke, Anglos and
Mexicans came running towards the shot, to see

what was happening. Choddi was raised in another school. When he heard a gun he hid and waited to see what happened next. As he was doing now.

Something kept pulling his attention to a ridge, off to the north-east, but it was too far to see properly. He wished he had a pair of the come-closer glasses that soldier chiefs used, that had magic glass in them to steal away distance and bring faraway things close up against the eye.

Another rifle sounded. And another.

Then came the buzzards. Choddi drank a mouthful of water from a skinbag, chewed a piece of jerked meat. He sucked a pebble. He listened to the shooting and watched the buzzards. Sometimes his thoughts drifted, to women and old times. Women had always been his trouble. He'd still be living a good life on the reservation, a scout on good pay, one of the agency police, if it hadn't been for the woman ... and her father, one of the Coyotero Apache peace chiefs. The old man had caught them together and Choddi had had to kill him too. And then he had run.

A louse fell from the Indian's strong black mane of hair and wriggled on to his left forearm. Choddi popped the crawler into his mouth. He rubbed the stock of the Henry which he'd studded with brass tacks and inspected the terrain before him. He had a good field of fire here and good cover. The mesquite grove was a good place to hide. But now he moved out of it, going forward over open ground....

SEVEN

Taylor found his place: nature had gouged a hole in the hillside. He could stand in it, hidden to the waist, and had placed a few substantial rocks in front of it as cover. No rocks behind him, fortunately; an enemy firing at him would try and glance ricochets off rocks into his hiding place. An angle of the mountains shielded him from the full force of the sun. And he had an excellent field of fire.

For a hundred yards below Taylor, the gradients were too steep for horsebackers. Below that, for about the same distance, the slope was easier, a rider could walk a horse up there, though they'd be wiser going afoot. A wide fan of gently rising ground at the base of the incline was fringed with cactus and mesquite trees. But anyone coming from the trees would have no real cover all the way to where Taylor sat, waiting. And his pursuers were riding through the timber now, on the threshold of the trap....

Taylor had stripped off his shirt as he didn't want any cloth driven into a wound. He'd folded his bandanna into a sweatband and bound it across his temples. Now he shrank down into his hole. He'd taken a blanket from the grey horse, covered it in sand and laid it over the front of the hole, almost concealing the spot. He ducked under this blanket and lifted the Spencer. He put the butt of the carbine out from under the blanket. The ammunition belt, the pistol, the gunbelt with nineteen shells in the loops, all lay close at hand. He swallowed and ran the tip of his tongue across his lips. His arms began to tremble and he willed them to be steady. His head ached, sweat was cold on his back and shoulders.

The three riders came from the trees.

They came single file. The leading horsebacker wore a faded blue US cavalry jacket and rode a paint horse. Taylor was fairly sure it was Griffin. Second was a black man in canvas jacket and shapeless hat, riding a rosewood bay. Bringing up the rear was a man on a sorrel horse. Taylor could make out few details of this man because of the haze; the rider took his hat from his head and showed red hair. All three riders were walking their horses in this heat; Griffin carried a rifle across his saddle.

Taylor took aim on Griffin's chest. He didn't know what condition the Spencer was in, how true the sighting; he knew shooting downhill was tricky, especially through a haze; but he was most concerned with mastering his own fear.

These men would kill him, unless he killed them first. Griffin had tied him to a wagon wheel, had laughed about the hard death they had in store for their prisoner, tied to an anthill, face up to the sun with his eyelids sliced away ... probably all three of these men had blood on their hands; they were all horsethieves, a crime with death as the only punishment. What had Griffin said about white men who 'lay with red bitches'? For all that, Taylor didn't know if he could do it, shoot men down like dogs, regardless of who they were, or what they'd done. Fear gouged into his stomach, made a high singing in his ears.

The knock of hooves on stones, the cough of a horse, brought him back from his thoughts. The riders had strung out he saw, the most distant well back towards the timber whilst Griffin was gently nudging his paint into steeper ground, only 150 yards distant, and the black man midway between his two companions.

Suddenly Griffin's horse reared.

The animal whinnied and swung about.

The Negro pulled the rifle from his saddle scabbard. He yelled.

Taylor drew a quick aim on Griffin.

He fired.

For a second he thought he'd missed entirely. Then the paint horse threw up its head and began to fall backwards.

Griffin sprang clear, he vanished over the off-side of the horse. The paint went down in a bursting cloud of dust. Behind him the Negro yelled and spurred his horse forward. Taylor fired at him, the horse stumbled and the black man pitched headfirst out of the saddle. He scrabbled about on his hands and knees, reeled dizzily to his feet. Taylor's next shot knocked him sprawling.

Taylor knew the third rider, the most distant horseman, was also moving. He was wheeling his horse about as if he was about to head for the cover of the trees he'd just left; instead he whirled his mount around in a complete circle and came towards Taylor. He yelled. Taylor shot him out of the saddle.

Taylor ducked at the crack of another rifle. Griffin's Springfield Long Tom.

The next time he dared raise his head, he looked for his enemies. Griffin's horse lay dead; the red-haired man sprawled in the open. Taylor knew he was dead too; another stranger the range detective had killed, without even seeing his face. He couldn't see either Griffin or the black man. He'd hit the latter, but how badly?

Time passed. A heat haze began to interfere with Taylor's view of the ground downslope.

Both horsethieves showed themselves. They lunged into the open, almost simultaneously, going left and right, running upslope. They sprang into cover. Taylor, who'd been offered only uncertain, bobbing targets in the haze, held his fire; his enemies would have to cross a lot of ground to get far enough upslope to have him outflanked. He noted that the wounded man had run awkwardly, his left shoulder thrust ahead of him, so perhaps he'd been hit there; the haze had prevented Taylor from seeing clearly.

The sky became a furnace, scoured of all colour by blinding waves of heat. Taylor's sandpit became a sweatbox and he sweated. But it was worse for the men downslope. They had no water, or overhead cover. They were lying on and between rocks that trapped the heat and reflected the sun's glare. It would soon be terrible for the wounded man. They were horsethieves, they'd ridden out today to murder *him* and for all that they were brave men, good at this game, better than most Anglos, Taylor could pity them, trapped on the slope in the eye of the pounding, desiccating sun.

An interested party gathered; a halo of buzzards. One after another they dipped their wings and planed down from the sky.

Griffin sprang to his feet and ran upslope. Taylor fired and missed. Griffin may have tripped; he went down on one shoulder and rolled. Taylor fired again too quickly and missed. He caught Griffin in his sights as the man sprawled wriggling between rocks. Taylor pulled the trigger and the Spencer jammed. He swore and worked at the hammer of the carbine and Griffin's body shot out of cover like a dustblue tongue, stretched and was gone.

Taylor swore, at his own panicked shooting, at the Spencer owner for not keeping the weapon in better repair; or perhaps at the dust that might have got into the gun's mechanism. But mostly at the Texan for getting where he was now. There was too much cover on that incline; brittlebrush, dwarf cholla trees, octillo. And from there Griffin had Taylor flanked, could get him in a crossfire, turn the ambush pit into a trap.

Once Taylor had worked the jammed cartridge from the breech of the Spencer, he moved. He pushed the Spencer carefully before him, slid over the lip of the pit, crawled on his belly and elbows. Griffin tried a shot at him and Taylor squirmed about and sqeezed the trigger; this time the Spencer fired. He kept moving, snaking into rock-strewn ground. Now, like his enemies, he felt the full force of the sun.

He bellied forward into meagre cover, jumping cholla gave little shade. From there he watched the nearest slopes. His opponents were *very* good at this game. He couldn't see either of them.

Soon, however, he began to hear the wounded man.

The man started calling something but Taylor couldn't make out the words. At first Taylor thought he might be singing deliriously, before he realized the man was shouting, a long string of curses. He also cried, 'I want water!'

From somewhere on the hillside, Griffin's disembodied voice came. 'Stick with it, Jubilee! We'll get this sonofabitch!'

But Jubilee kept shouting: 'I want water! I ain't in this no more!' He shouted until his voice was cracked and hoarse. Taylor tried to close his ears to the yelling, wearing away at his nerves.

A rifle flipped from cover, spun and clattered on rocks. Jubilee cried, 'I ain't in this!'

The man stood. He swayed, one hand to his left shoulder. There was blood on his canvas jacket, his jeans. He stared upslope, his eyes wild, his mouth open, gasping for air. He turned jerkily and began to walk downslope. He slid on to his rump, slithered three yards, pushed himself back to his feet and began to pick his way downhill.

The dust-fouled back of his canvas jacket swam into focus above the Spencer's front sights. Taylor had a spot picked midway between Jubilee's shoulders. He told himself, I ain't in this either, and squeezed carefully.

The afternoon grew hotter. The desert lay copper and sterile under haze and sky; nothing moved but the buzzards, scrabbling in the dust.

Taylor glimpsed another movement in the tail of his eye; the slanting flight of a cactus wren. The bird swung towards a clump of jumping cholla. At the last moment the wren flared its brown wings, veered away. Taylor lay his cheek against the gunstock and studied a pile of rocks behind the cholla clump. There was a gap in this pile. Suddenly the gap turned blue; When Griffin reared up behind the rocks and sprang forward, Taylor was ready for him. He fired. Griffin somersaulted headlong, crashed on his back across stones. Dust rose. The Texan rolled, he sat up, one hand pressed to his side. He lifted the hand, laughed in shock and pain.

The Texan was down only fifty yards from Taylor. The range detective took his time aiming, fixed Griffin's chest in his sights. He squeezed the trigger and the Spencer jammed. Taylor swore, worked the lever. Still jammed!

Griffin got to his knees, reached for the Springfield.

Taylor dropped the Spencer, got to his feet and launched himself from the rocks. He ran downhill, towards Griffin. He glimpsed the Texan on one knee, throwing the butt of the Springfield into one shoulder. Taylor swerved, coming in on the rifleman in a series of zigzags, Apache style. Griffin drove a shot at the weaving runner and missed. The horsethief swore and grabbed a fresh cartridge. He flicked back the breech flap and ejected the used shell, dropped in the new cartridge, clashed the block shut, rammed back the side hammer and Taylor leapt. He drove his left shoulder hard into the Texan's chest and both men went down.

They scrambled upright. Still on one knee, Griffin lifted his rifle by the barrel. Taylor kicked him in the throat. Griffin fell on his side, hands to his throat, gasping. Slowly, he got to his knees.

Taylor waited, the Springfield in his hands. As Griffin stood, Taylor hit him in the stomach with the barrel of the rifle. The Texan doubled forward, went to his knees. Taylor took time to judge the next blow; he struck crosswise with the butt of the Springfield. Griffin toppled, lay face down.

Taylor sat on the earth. He found he was gasping for air, sweat ran from him, his arms were shaking. After a time, he managed to stand and gazed at Griffin. The blow to the head had been a terrible one but the Texan was still breathing. Taylor pointed the Springfield at the prone figure. He only had to squeeze the trigger once ... he thought about the other horsethief, Jubilee....

He took the rag from around his head and tied it around his throat. He took Jubilee's rifle, which was a Winchester 'Yellowboy'. He glanced briefly at the dead man. How many corpses in this business so far? Four, five? He scowled and began to walk back upslope, to where he'd ground-hitched the grey horse. Above him a late-coming buzzard swooped to join its fellows, tawny wings wide, its eye a stony, hungry gleaming.

EIGHT

The buzzards flared their wings; Choddi had to swipe at them with the barrel of his rifle before they left their feeding. They rose into the air, protesting, their harsh cries wearing at his nerves. They'd been feeding on the black/white man, they'd already torn his face into a ruin not even Choddi, with his strong stomach, could look at. The Indian noted that the man's Winchester was missing.

Off to the north, other buzzards fought over Dutch Charlie. Griffin lay nearby; Choddi noticed the rise and fall of the unconscious man's chest. Taylor could have killed the soldier but he hadn't; Choddi wondered at that.

The tracks of the horse with the lame right forehoof pointed north. Choddi began to follow them. He went forward warily, thinking about Jubilee's good rifle, now in Taylor's hands. Behind him the buzzards returned to feeding on Taylor's handiwork. No wonder, Choddi thought, even his own people were afraid of this strange, dark Anglo, who'd lived amongst them and in some ways become as much Apache as any of them, the Shadow Man....

* * *

Taylor rode north from the killing place on the limping grey. He had a stroke of luck; he came across Jubilee's rosewood bay, feet tangled in its lines. He mounted the animal and rode out its initial resistance to a new owner. He now had a sound horse under him. He rode north, now was the time to put distance between himself and pursuit.

At nightfall he camped in a canyon. He estimated he was only five or so miles south of the American line. When he crossed the border he'd either be on the Papago Reservation or on the Turkey Track ranch. Ben Shields owned the Turkey Track; he was one of the most important ranchers in southern Arizona. Taylor had never met him as he wasn't one of the range detective's collective employers.

Early next morning, Taylor got moving again. After a few miles he came out of the canyon country on to the desert. He struck a wash with a narrow trickle of water moving along the bottom. At its deepest the water only came as high as the horse's knees, and the bay crossed it in twenty strides. An insignificant little watercourse, except that Taylor entered it from Mexico and came out of it in Arizona. He knew he was now on Ben Shield's land.

Something was making him nervous. He had a feeling he was still being followed but it didn't make any sense that the horsethieves would pursue him this far. Nonetheless, he trusted his instincts. He rode warily up the next ridge and halted just before the summit, so that he could see over,

without being outlined against the sky. This part of
Arizona was called the 'tree desert'. It wasn't bare
sand, like some deserts, but thickly vegetated land,
covered in chaparral, cactus and a riot of fiendishly
spiked, thorny plants. Heat-haze made visibility
even more difficult. Taylor needed his army field
glasses to see properly, but some horsethief had
them now, back in the Canyon Of The Dead.
Taylor scrutinized the terrain before him for a few
minutes without seeing anything amiss, but he
knew a whole army could be hiding within half a
mile of him and he'd never see them. He also gave
himself the luxury of admiring the country. Many
Anglos found this landscape harsh, alien and
primitive but this was Taylor's world, he loved it,
he didn't suppose he could ever leave it now.

He rode downslope, through a maze of saguaro
and mesquite. He approached a low saddle, a notch
between two hills. The saddle was covered in palo
verde trees.

Taylor reined in the bay.

There was a wink of bright metal in the trees.

Hooves clattered on a bed of stones. Two
horsemen came from the palo verdes. One of the
riders had a rifle in his hand.

Taylor heard more hooves behind him, he
judged two horsemen had ridden from the
chaparral behind him. Another man appeared
atop the giant boulder before Taylor and to his
left, thus completing the trap. The man on the
boulder pointed his rifle at Taylor.

The range detective sat still. If the newcomers
were horsethieves out of the robbers' roost, he was
a dead man, it would all end here and now. But
they might be Turkey Track riders patrolling the

border, on the lookout for smugglers, wetbacks and stockthieves crossing from Mexico.

Taylor turned his head slowly. The two riders behind him were walking their horses towards him. The horsemen in the palo verdes were riding forward. They were both Anglos, they looked like better-off than average cowboys. One was still in his teens, just starting on his first pale beard. He slid the rifle he held back into the saddle scabbard. Taylor was pleased about that, he didn't like guns in the hands of excitable youths. The other man was about thirty, dressed like a top hand.

Taylor asked, 'You Turkey Track riders?'

The older man nodded. He took off his sombrero and wiped sweat from his forehead with his sleeve. He was handsome in a cold, unsmiling way, with receding yellow hair and burnsides. He was clean shaven. He said, 'That's right.' His voice made him southern, maybe Texan. 'I'm Print Henry.'

Taylor grunted recognition at the name. He'd been right: Print Henry was Ben Shields' top hand. He felt some of the tension and weariness ease out of him. The range detective leaned forward in the saddle. He said, 'I've heard about you. I was—'

He heard the rope in the air. A noose fell over his head and shoulders. The rope was pulled tight, pinning his arms to his sides and jerking him backwards. He was yanked from the saddle and struck the earth on his runp with an impact that jarred the teeth in his head. He sat, half-winded. His horse jumped forward but before it could run the boy with Henry had lifted a rope from his saddle, expertly he cast a noose over the animal's neck.

Henry said, 'Good throw, Ike.'

Taylor got to his feet, slowly and painfully. The rope that held him was tugged, he was jolted backwards and he went back on his rump. One of the men behind him laughed. He saw the boy, Ike, grinning. Taylor sighed and got to his feet again. He turned and looked at the man holding the rope, a blocky shape astride a chestnut horse. He recognized him now: the Grant County lawman, Pete Olsen.

'Well looky here,' said Olsen. 'We got us a horsethief.' He pulled the carbine from the boot on his saddle. It was a Remington-Keene repeater.

The rider with Olsen was another boy, perhaps sixteen. He was tall and gangling with a fierce thatch of red hair and a thin, deeply freckled face. He sat a paint horse. Taylor saw the boy was holding the paint on a tight rein. It looked a good cutting horse, a horse that could jump forwards or sideways at the touch of a rein, or the pressure of a rider's knee on the flank. The horse was tensed now, ready to jump, nostrils flared, eyes red. The rider was tensed too, eager to do something, his grin too fixed, his eyes wild. Taylor was reminded of the horsethief, Anders. He remembered Anders slamming against him, dead in his arms. The other boy, Ike, had the same excitement in his face. It seemed to be Taylor's week for meeting unstable youths with weapons in their hands. He was frightened; nothing frightened him as much as guns in the hands of nervous men.

Olsen asked, 'Hey, Taylor, where's that horse you stole off me?'

'I didn't steal it.'

'Where is it now?'

'Them horsethieves still got it.'

Olsen's face coloured with anger. 'Truth is, you're in with them horsethieves ain't you?'

Taylor said, 'You're crazy—'

The red-haired boy shifted in the saddle; his horse leapt forward. Taylor began to spring sideways but was too slow. The chest of the horse caught him half turning and flung him backwards. He struck the earth on his shoulders, he lay still, hearing the wind go out of his lungs. Bright flashing colours got mixed up with his vision. The redhead spun the paint about neatly and rode back towards Olsen, his back stiff with arrogance. Ike yelled and whooped. He called, 'You show him, Red!'

Red swung the paint round again, as if he intended to repeat his trick. His freckled face was cracked in a wild-eyed, not quite sane, grin. He said, 'Let's string up this horsethief!'

Olsen lifted his rifle. 'You don't need a rope for their kind.'

Print Henry said, 'Hold up there, Olsen. Rein that horse in, Red.'

The boy glared at the top hand. 'Aw, come on, Print. Lawman here says this is a horsethief—'

'Stole his horse, he says!' Ike cried.

Henry slid his sombrero back on his head. 'We'll let Mister Shields decide all that, once he gets the facts.'

Olsen sneered, 'Facts!'

Red sneered too. 'Facts!'

Henry nodded slowly. 'That's how we do things round here.'

Once again, Taylor climbed slowly to his feet. Henry told him, 'Get on that horse.'

Olsen ran his rifle back in the saddle scabbard.
'All right, we'll take him to your boss. We'll get the
facts. And then we'll hang him.'

Taylor climbed aboard the rosewood bay. Ike
tied his feet together under the horse's belly. He
tied the captive's wrists to the saddlehorn. Taylor
wondered if his wrists would start to ache soon if
there wasn't a rope tied around them.

Red glared. He asked petulantly, 'Ain't there
gonna be a hanging? Ain't we gonna string that
horsethief up?'

Olsen took the reins of Taylor's horse, leading
the animal. 'Shut up, kid,' he said.

NINE

Calvin Taylor stood by the window and watched the rain.

There was a dog outside, sitting under a wagon, sheltering from the rain. A grey-white mongrel, with one black eye patch. When he was a boy, about ten years old, Taylor had a dog something like that mongrel; a bitch, he remembered, but he couldn't recall her name or what had happened to her.

Looking past the wagon he could see buildings – adobe sheds, outbuildings, the bunkhouse, the Shields' ranch house. The latter was a particularly impressive building, with two storeys and three wings; it might once have been the chapel of a renovated Spanish mission. A low adobe wall ran around the building, moonlight gleamed on the black wrought-iron grilling of various gateways.

The dog stretched, began to chew at one of its forepaws.

Taylor said, 'Got some sheepdog in her.'

'Uh?'

'That bitch out there. Got some sheepdog in her.'

Charlie Free laid the tin plate he'd been eating off on the earth and stood. He had a Winchester trapped between his side and his right arm. He was a tall man, about Taylor's height. He wore a faded blue shirt, a red knot and dip bandanna, cord jacket, battered levis. He had a single-action Army Colt holstered on the front of his right thigh. He wasn't a young man, he looked at least forty. He asked Taylor, 'True you run with Indians?'

Taylor fingered the last few beans on the tin plate into his mouth and wiped his lips with the back of his wrist. Eating was no problem for his hands weren't bound. It was moving around that was difficult.

Charlie asked, 'True that Indians think a sight of black skin?'

Taylor lifted both feet eighteen inches above the earth. That was about all he could manage; the iron fetters on his ankles were on a short chain, about a yard long. The last link was bent under a stakepin sledged into the earth. At full stretch, lying on his belly, Taylor could touch three walls of this adobe but not the fourth, where the steerhide door was. Charlie Free stood between Taylor and the door.

Taylor asked, 'Where'd you get these damn leg irons?'

'You're honoured. Them chains ain't been wore for twenty years. I know. I was the last to wear 'em before you?'

'You were a slave?'

'Hell no! I used to be President of The United States! Was I a slave?' Charlie laughed harshly. 'I was Ben Shields' personal slave!'

Charlie fashioned a cigarette and lifted the kerosene lamp to light it, so that the room rocked briefly between a half-darkness of looming shadows and sallow glare of the lamp. He was a light-skinned black man, like someone else Taylor had met recently. Thinking of that, Taylor scowled and stared at the earth a moment. He said, 'Those sons of bitches kept you chained up like this, yet you still stick with 'em?'

The other man shaped another cigarette, he threw this and his strike-a-light across to Taylor. 'I grew up with Mister Shields. His pappy, George, bought me. I had a home. Where else would I go?'

'You were a slave.'

'And somewhere else I'd be free? They called me Charlie Free; that makes me free? Ain't nobody free, or wants to be!'

'They put irons on you.'

'Everybody got irons on them, one kind or another.' Charlie drank coffee from a tin cup. 'There's worst things than being a slave. Leastways a slave gets looked after.' He coughed over his cigarette. 'Twenty years, nearly, Mister George been dead. He weren't much over fifty but this country – Texas too – uses a man up fast. Riding horses busts up your innards and the land just wears you out.'

'I don't know. If anybody kept me like this ... I'd go crazy.'

Charlie sneered, 'Sure you would. You'd learn to hold it in, Taylor, just like I had to.'

'Would I? There's some Indians, down in Mexico, they got to be slaves, mission Indians; but there were others, like the Apaches ... they'd die before you could make a slave out of them.'

'That's because Apaches ain't human men. They're wild animals. You'd think different, o'course.'

Horseshoes slapped mud. Taylor stood, heeled his cigarette, stamped his feet (with difficulty because of the irons) and rubbed his palms along the gnawing stiffness in his calves. He gazed through the window-hole, a meagre opening too small to climb through. The dog was gone. Three horsemen came from the darkness, drew rein outside the adobe. The riders dismounted in slackening rain and crowded into the doorway. Charlie Free let them in. The newcomers took off their slickers and shook rain from them. Print Henry and Pete Olsen and a man he didn't know. A very large man. This man said, 'Go get coffee, Charlie.'

Mechanically the Negro answered, 'Yes sir.' He left.

The large man stripped fringed gauntlets from his hands. He said, 'I'm Benjamin Shields.'

Shields wore something like a frock coat. Taylor wasn't certain of the colour of his hair as Shields was standing back from the light but it might be light brown, with some grey in it. He had a fierce chin beard but no burnsides or moustaches; this, his eyes, which had a wild look to them, his grim mouth, his bulk, gave him the aspect of some unforgiving Old Testament preacher glowering down on a sinful world. A man who could carve a kingdom for himself out of the wilderness of Apacheria, who could turn a man between his hands like a twist of rope. Someone, Taylor thought, who kept hold of the slave chains his family owned, perhaps as a reminder of a time when his kind had the power to shackle other people like animals and buy and sell their freedom.

Shields said, 'I've heard of you, Taylor.' His accent, Taylor judged, might have its origins in east Texas.

Taylor said, 'Ditto.'

'You want to tell your side of it?'

'You know what I do. I was doing it.'

'I've heard bits of what you're supposed to do. Run guns to Apache renegades. Live with greasers. Fornicate with heathen Indian squaws. Murder innocent cowboys and make it look like they were stealing stock.'

Taylor said, 'You forgot to mention I eat babies raw.'

Print Henry gave a short grunt. He moved his right hand to his side. A quirt hung by a loop from his waistband, Henry touched it briefly. Perhaps the man had plaited the leather of the quirt himself. If so, he'd done a good job of it. He said, 'You watch your mouth, Taylor.'

Olsen sneered, 'He's got a mouth on him, all right.'

Shields added to his fire-and-brimstone preacher-look by quoting from the Bible: ' *"A fool's mouth is his destruction; and his lips are the snare of his soul"*.'

Taylor was angry; he realized it was because of the irons around his ankles and that he needed to control his temper. He said, 'I was doing what I'm paid for. What I don't understand is—' Suddenly his temper had hold of him and he didn't care. 'Why I'm in these goddamn irons!'

Olsen shaped a cigarette. 'There's a matter of a horse you stole. And that greaser horsethief that got free.'

'He's the one who stole your horse.'

'You tied his hands, how come he got loose?'

'In case you forgot, Olsen, I shot that horsethief and killed another.'

'That's what you and Beckwirth told me. Maybe it was a story you three all worked out between you.'

'And the *charro* let himself get shot or something? Bullshit.'

Shields quoted the Tenth Psalm: ' "*The wicked through the pride of his countenance will not seek after God … his mouth is full of cursing, deceit and fraud; under his tongue is mischief and vanity*".'

Shields had obviously put in some time as a stump preacher and had never got out of the habit; he'd been good at it too, Taylor guessed; he had the eyes for it. Eyes that judged and condemned, a stare to wither all the sinful. While Print Henry's eyes were a cold, washed-out blue, the ranch-owner's eyes were a deep rosewood brown, only tips of fire glimmered at their core.

Shields said, 'In a few days I'll be meeting with some of the men who may be employing you. Then we'll find out what's going on.'

'In the meantime, you keep me chained like an animal....'

'I don't sit still while thieves rob my herds, Taylor. You smell wrong to me. You smell like a thief to me.'

'Do I?'

Print Henry stepped forward, one hand to the butt of the quirt. Shields said, 'Wait a minute, Henry.' He glared at Taylor. 'I lost close to four hundred head of stock to thieves this winter. I can't afford to let that happen. I have a reputation to maintain. "*To me belongeth vengeance and recompence. If I whet my glittering sword and mine hand take hold on judgement, I will render vengeance to mine enemies and will reward them that hate me!*" '

In other circumstances, the rancher might have looked and sounded comic and preposterous, but the eyes changed that, the eyes of a hunting bird, with a hint of madness in the stare, that, and the bull-like strength of the man. Shields said, 'Where I was raised, we hanged horsethieves as the lowest things living. That was Texas, forty years gone. Nothing's changed.'

Olsen asked, 'Just who is employing you, Taylor?'

'Pima County Stockman's Association. Look, Shields, you want to find those thieves, I can tell you where to look. I found their roost.'

Henry said, 'Where?'

'Fifty miles south of the border. Dead Man's Canyon.'

Shields said, 'I hope you don't think you're dealing with fools, Taylor.'

'You don't believe me, take a look down there yourself.'

Shields pulled on his gauntlets, wrapped his slicker around his shoulders. He told Henry, 'You watch him till the old Nigger gets back.'

'I'll watch him,' Olsen volunteered.

Taylor hoped Shields would object, but he didn't. Shields and Henry left. Olsen leaned against the wall and made another cigarette. Taylor supposed the other man was thinking about the blow he'd got on the head and the bayo coyote horse he'd lost. He might want to get some of his own back by taking it out on Taylor, now the latter was pegged to the earth like a tethered goat.

Olsen said, 'I want that horse back, Taylor.' Anger built in his voice. 'No one makes a fool out of me.'

Taylor gazed out of the window-hole. Olsen observed, 'So you work for Pima County Stockman's Association. How much they pay you to steal their stock?'

TEN

Calvin Taylor woke before dawn the next morning, a habit that had kept him alive, before today, in Apache country. He heard hands riding out. Work started before cock crow here, as on most ranches. The early light showed him the layout of the place. Apart from the usual structures – the main house, blacksmith's shop, tack shed, wagonsheds, bunkhouse, commissary, stables – there were a scattering of huts and adobes. Already the ranch was more nearly a village; Shields had certainly put his mark on this country.

Charlie Free brought Taylor a meagre breakfast and watched him eat it. Then they smoked. About mid morning, Taylor saw a vehicle approaching the ranch from the north. It was a stage-coach; nothing unusual about that, as stages often used ranches as waystations along the road; except this vehicle was painted blood red and all the metal on the coach down to the trace chains, was polished until the shining hurt the eye, an act of folly or bravado in this wilderness, with bandits and perhaps even wild Indians at large.

The stage halted by the main ranch building. The one passenger climbed from the vehicle. Or rather Print Henry helped her from the coach, his hat in his other hand, his manner properly deferential. The woman wore dark clothing, a heavy, ankle-length skirt, hemmed with barlead, all of which must be torture to wear in this heat. A wide-brimmed hat, decked with a ribbon, shaded her face; her hair, pinned back at the nape, was, as far as Taylor could tell, dark or dark red. He guessed she was about twenty-five.

Taylor said, 'Beautiful woman.'

Charlie Free glanced out of the window-hole. Both men watched as Henry led the woman to a gateway in the wall about the main buildings, and through it, out of sight.

Charlie said, 'Mister Shields, he'd tear your throat out, he heard you say that.'

'Why? The old bastard possessive of his daughter?'

Charlie frowned. 'You don't order your daughters out of a Monkey Ward catalogue.' His expression changed; he smiled faintly at the puzzled look Taylor gave him. 'She ain't his daughter. She's his wife.'

Taylor slept through the worst of the day's heat. It was a troubled sleep and he dreamed. He had an old dream, one that hadn't visited him in years. He was looking at a place in the mountains that was very familiar to him, although he couldn't remember where it was; somewhere in the Sierra Anchas perhaps. Apaches were there, Nah-Lin amongst them. She was just standing there, watching other Apache women dance the marriage dance. Was there a tumpline across her breast, a cradleboard on her back, a baby sleeping in the cradleboard, Nachay, whose name meant Rat...?

He looked for the small face, less plump and paler-skinned than the faces of other Apache babies....

He woke late in the afternoon. Charlie Free came over with another meal. They were fashioning their first smokes, Taylor was thinking about his dream; had it been Shields' woman who brought back memories of Nah-Lin? Something struck the adobe door. A voice outside said, 'It's Henry.'

Charlie stood, his Winchester cradled in his arms. He said, 'Mister Henry?' Taylor, heard the alarm in his voice and wondered what he was afraid of. Maybe some of Shields' hands were talking about settling Taylor themselves ... let him try and escape and deal with him *rurales*-style; or just lynch him from the nearest cottonwood. Olsen might be putting them up to it.

Taylor said, 'It's Henry, all right. Hear them spurs? Neither do I. Not much jingle-jangle on them Mexican belly scratchers.'

Free nodded. The Mexican spurs Henry wore gave little sound.

Something – probably the butt of a plaited leather quirt – rapped hard on the door again.

Charlie said, 'All right, Mister Henry.'

He opened the door. Print Henry entered, then Shields' wife. Taylor's mouth twisted with distaste at the look she gave the black man and the way Charlie took off his hat and ducked his head. He said, 'Ma'am.'

Henry told him, 'They need you over at the main house, Charlie.'

'Yessir.' Charlie left.

Taylor wondered if he was being too hard on

Charlie; he couldn't know how much a black man had to crawl to survive out here.

Henry said, 'Get up.'

Taylor took his time complying, not through insolence but because his legs had very little strength in them. He was surprised how weak he felt. He had to put his back against the wall to keep upright.

Henry said, 'You'd best stay over there, ma'am.'

The woman smiled. She was beautiful, Taylor decided. Her face had an out-of-the-sun paleness with large, dark, poignant eyes; a sad, lovely face that belonged in a cameo, not in this wild, primitive country. But the smile changed her face, took away some of the vulnerability. She wore a dark dress with brown velvet buttons, silk trimmed overskirt, standing collar. Ladies didn't show their footwear or their ankles but she revealed both, having hitched her underskirt up out of the dust. She was wearing black kid boots. She held a folding fan she didn't make much play with, which was surprising; Taylor didn't know how she could stand this heat, in all those clothes. To Henry she said, 'Is he that dangerous?'

Taylor blinked at the mockery in the woman's voice. He supposed he looked like something the cat dragged in, his hair tangled, his face dark with stubble. You could trail his clothing – shirt, moccasins, levis – through five miles of dust and not make them appreciably shabbier.

Henry smiled too. He said, 'This is an animal. Squaw lover. Lives with savages. Got to be more Apache than white man.'

Taylor couldn't hold his temper, he said, 'That's right. Why, I even scared a long streak of piss like you, Henry.' This was childish, he knew, but he didn't care.

Henry's smile vanished. Not at the insult, but at the language. In the hard male world of the frontier you kept talk clean around women, or else the poor delicate things might faint away. Anglo women that is; no one would expect such a response from Mexican or Indian women.

Taylor squatted down, hands hanging between his knees, he tried to smile insolently.

The woman didn't faint at the obscenity. Instead it seemed to add to her amusement. She asked Henry, 'Are you going to let him talk to you like that?'

Henry's answer was to take one step forward, hands bunched into fists.

Taylor ducked as if he was cowering, then pushed himself upright, opening his hands, palms upwards. Some of the dust he'd grabbed from the earth went in Henry's face. The tophand swore and swung away, one arm barred across his eyes. That gave Taylor the chance to launch the one good punch he'd been saving, with all his strength behind it; but it landed on Henry's right cheek without any impact at all. Henry grunted and caught Taylor on the jaw with a right cross. Taylor slammed back against the wall and slid down to his rump, burning flesh off his back. He managed to climb upright once again. Henry waited, smiling. When Taylor got to his full height, Henry knocked him down again. After that, all Taylor could manage was to fold his arms around the other's legs. Henry kneed him in the belly and broke his hold. He grabbed a fistful of Taylor's hair and twisted the prisoner's face upwards. Henry's right fist went back to his shoulder.

Taylor glimpsed the woman's face; she was smiling a tight, breathless smile, her poignant eyes gleaming with excitement. He thought, I'm glad someone else is enjoying this.

Henry changed his mind about the punch he was aiming. Instead he moved his hand to his waist. His fingers hinged about the finely worked butt of the quirt; he lifted the quirt above his head.

ELEVEN

Ike lay face down on a small hillock, staring over the summit at the land to the east. Heat haze blurred visibility that way, as the mountains wavered and shimmered, like things seen through a rippling film of liquid, but the boy could just make out a horseman, riding across the cactus-stippled flats; he was coming towards the hillock.

Ike glanced over his right shoulder. Behind him, at the base of the hillock was a bosky of smoketrees, surrounding a small rock pool. Red was hiding there, by the pool – which were called tanks out here. He'd also hidden their horses in the bosk. The boys weren't hiding from horsethieves or hostile Indians or for any legitimate cause. They were hiding because Red had a jug of whiskey.

Ben Shields didn't allow liquor on his ranch. A suggestion of alcohol on a rider's breath would get him sacked. So the boys drank with a tremendous sense of their own daring at breaching this most fundamental of all Shields' rules, at their own mad disobedience. But they were careful not to drink too much. Whiskey took them too easily and didn't mix with either the day's heat or the gait of a cow pony.

Ike came slithering down from his lookout place

on the hillock to join Red, who passed him the jug. Ike drank; Red watched, his eyes narrowed and envious.

Ike wiped his mouth with the back of his wrist, as he'd seen his elders and betters do. He told Red, 'That horseman. It's Olsen, all right.'

'Jesus!' Red declared. 'He's an ugly one, ain't he?'

The other youth nodded vigorously. 'I'll say!' He spilled a little of the whiskey, which splashed on to the front of his blue shield-front shirt. He swore at that, it was his one good, go-to-town shirt.

Red laughed nastily. 'You're supposed to drink it, not take a bath in it!'

Ike laughed also, uneasily. He was a little frightened of Red. He summarized Olsen's physical appearance, 'He's got a face like a pig's ass!'

The boys laughed.

Turning his face to the east, Ike shouted at the out-of-earshot rider, 'Hey, Olsen! You got a face like a pig's ass!'

More laughter.

Ike studied the jug, deciding he was too scared to drink any more and wondering if Red might bully him into it. He said, 'That Olsen. He's a mean one, ain't he?'

'Real easy on the shoot, they say.'

'Yeah?'

'That's right. Straight as an arrow, but all mankiller.'

Ike thought a moment, deciding the whiskey wasn't helping him to do that, even though he'd only had a little of the stuff. He chose what was his favourite obscenity of the moment. 'He's a—!'

Red nodded. 'He's a real—!'

'That Taylor, he's a— too!'

Both boys scowled, thinking about Taylor.

Olsen rode into earshot. Red hid the jug in his saddle, both boys attempted to smile at the newcomer without guilt showing on their faces. If he knew about the jug, the lawman might sneak on them to Shields ... they had worked out a cover story, they'd taken shelter in the bosky to rest their overheated horses.

Red said, 'Hot day.'

Olsen reined in his horse. He declared, 'Too hot for riding.'

He dismounted and walked over to the tank. He dipped his hands into the rock pool and splashed water on to his face, then on to his neck. He said, 'Aaaahhhh!' He let his horse drink then soaked his bandanna, wringing out the cloth over his head, so the water ran into his hair and down his face. He said, 'Aaaahhhh!'

Red smirked and glanced at Ike. Ike smirked too, he began to laugh, swallowing the laughter although it swelled out his cheeks. He stared at the earth, put his hands over his mouth and his face reddened; he managed to turn the laughter into a series of barking coughs. But Olsen hadn't noticed a thing, carried on wringing out the bandanna over his upturned face.

He asked, 'You boys join me?' He produced a bottle. 'Mexican liquor. Pulque.'

The boys stared.

Olsen said, "Course I know it ain't allowed, but....'

Ike said, 'We already got us a jug.'

Olsen smiled. 'I know. I seen.' He lifted a pair of army field glasses.

The boys gaped. For a second both forgot that with field glasses the mankiller could see much further than he could hear. He couldn't have heard their comments on his appearance ... after a moment, both youths returned fixed smiles to their faces. Red took his jug from his saddle and offered it to Olsen. The lawman sniffed the bottle and drank. He made a face and spat. 'You can't drink this stuff! Anybody here drink a real man's drink?'

Ike and Red both decided they were real men; they said, 'Yes!' simultaneously.

Olsen handed over the bottle; he rolled a smoke while the boys drank. He said, 'You know, I don't understand how you do things around here.'

Red had drunk from the bottle; now he stared at it suspiciously, astonished at the strength of the liquor. 'Oh?'

'Take that horsethief, Taylor. Up in Grant County we'd've handled him different. We'd've just looked round for the nearest tree. Only one law for horsethieves round there.'

Red said, 'Same here! We got the same law here. That's what I wanted to do when we first caught him. Remember? That's what I wanted to do!'

Ike nodded. 'That's right!' He offered the bottle to Olsen.

The lawman shook his head. 'You get outside of that bottle, boys. 'Course, it's a real man's drink, so could be it's a little too hairy for you....'

Red grinned. 'Pass her over!'

Ike said, 'Me next!'

Olsen let the boys pass the bottle between themselves a few more times before he said, 'Yes, we should have strung up that horsethief then and there!'

Red nodded. 'That's what I said. Ain't it? That's what I said!'

Olsen studied his cigarette. 'Well, talk's kind of cheap.'

'Whadderyoumean?'

'There's talking and doing.'

Red spent a moment looking at Olsen; he felt uneasy now, suspicious of the half-gloating look on the lawman's face and of the liquor that was warm and dizzy in his head. 'I told you, I wanted to string Taylor up!'

Ike said, 'That's right! You did!'

'What's stopping you then, Red? What's stopping either of you?'

There was a silence, the boys stared owlishly at the older man. Finally, Red said, 'There's a guard. That old Nigger....'

'He can be took care of. He don't have to be hurt or nothin'....'

Ike said, 'I don't like this.'

Olsen sneered, 'You don't, huh? Like I said, talk's cheap.'

'If anyone was to try and lynch Taylor, why, Shields, why....' For a moment Ike was at a loss for words. 'He'd have their hide!'

'He'd never find out who done it. A pair of gunnysackers....' Olsen shrugged. ''Course that kind of thing takes sand. If you ain't got the guts....'

Red leaned forward, bending so low he bumped his chin on his kneecap. He asked, 'If we was to go for it ... just how would you get past Charlie Free?'

'There's ways.'

Red lowered his voice, whispering like a conspirator, 'How?'

Olsen smiled.

* * *

Choddi smiled also. With bitterness. He hated to see good liquor go to waste, that is, be consumed by other men. Like those three white-eyes, lounging in the shade by the tank. He studied them now through Dutch Charlie's comes-closer glasses. He could have sworn. Not in Apache, there was no profanity in his own language. To swear he had to use the language of the white-eyes and yellow-eyes, the Americans and Mexicans.

Choddi had dug a hole for himself in the earth and huddled there now, half-covered by his blanket. He'd hidden himself in a good place, a place where enemies wouldn't look for him. Anglos and Mexicans looked for enemies in places with plenty of cover, but an Apache, if he was skillful enough, would hide himself in a bald, open spot where no searching eye would tarry.

Choddi lifted the field glasses to his eyes once more, inspected the men by the tank. He might have killed two men for a jug of good liquor – he could pick them off easily with his good rifle from where he lay – but three was a different proposition. When he got killed, he decided, it would be for a better reason than that ... for now, he was happy just to watch, and wait his time.

TWELVE

'You want coffee?'

Charlie Free's voice pulled Taylor back from his thoughts. 'What?'

The Negro said, 'You want coffee? We got Mocha and Java, Mocha and Java or Mocha and Java.'

'Well, I ain't picky. You choose.'

Charlie poured coffee into a tin cup. 'Prefer Mojav coffee myself.'

It was full dark outside. A kerosene lamp lit the adobe interior; Free and Taylor were in a circle of dim yellow light. The wind that had shrieked like a legion of lost souls all day had gentled; now it sounded like a couple of badly tuned whorehouse pianos rattling along together.

Charlie squatted a yard beyond Taylor's reach, his battered Winchester laid across his knees.

Someone kicked the door. A voice, outside, said, 'Print Henry.'

In a low voice, Taylor said, 'Hey, Charlie. Hear them spurs? So do I.'

Charlie gave the prisoner a frightened look. He asked, 'You alone, Mister Henry?'

'Sure, what the hell?' Taylor listened; the wind and the door's thickness might be playing tricks with his hearing but there was something in the voice that didn't sound right.

Charlie stood, staring at the door, gripping the Winchester. He said, 'I dunno, Mister Henry.'

Taylor whispered, 'I ain't worth getting killed for, Charlie.'

Another voice, high and young, came: 'Let us in!'

The older voice said, 'You open up now, Charlie. You'll be all right. Otherwise you get it with the prisoner. Your choice.'

The young voice said, 'Let us in you old Nigger.'

Charlie walked a quick circle, took one step backwards, said, 'I dunno—' and Taylor sprang. His linked hands went over Charlie's head. Taylor was pulled short by the leg irons; he skidded to his knees. In falling, he yanked Charlie backwards. The man did a complete backwards somersault and landed on all fours. Taylor grabbed Charlie's ears. He bowed his forehead almost to the earth and smashed his head into Charlie's face and went on his back, half-stunned himself. Charlie rocked back on his haunches, bloody-faced, his mouth gaping. Taylor hooked an elbow into the other's throat and the man fell sideways, hands under his chin. Taylor wrestled the Colt from the holster on Charlie's right thigh. Charlie rammed a knee under Taylor's chin with force enough to clash his teeth together. Taylor cracked the Negro across the shinbone with the barrel of the pistol. Charlie's leg kicked out in a wild nervelessness and he would have screamed if Taylor hadn't already driven his throat apple into his windpipe. Taylor lunged forward, lashing out with the gun barrel and sending the kerosene lamp spinning and wiping out the light as the steerhide door flew open. A man filled the doorway. Taylor fired the Colt and drove him backwards. From the doorway a pistol flamed. Taylor fired into the muzzle flash, the two guns sounding almost as one.

For a few seconds Taylor was blinded by the muzzle flash. He heard a clamour of excited voices, running feet. A horse screamed. A voice just outside the door yelled, 'What the hell's going on?' Taylor recognized Print Henry's voice, this time the real article.

A figure holding a lamp above his head flickered into the doorway. He tripped over something on the threshold and fell forward; he dropped the lamp and the adobe was back in darkness. A huddle of figures blundered around in the entrance, voices swore and grumbled, then a match flared.

Taylor flung the handgun across the room and raised his hands.

He thought, what if I've killed Charlie Free?

Lamps were lit. Pistols and rifles were being flourished. Print Henry elbowed his way into the adobe. He was thumbing up the buttons of his undershirt. His thin, flaxen hair was awry, his cheeks were flushed. Taylor thought, he looks like he's just been at it, has he got a woman hid out around here?

Charlie Free was still alive. He began to cry out, hoarsely, that his shin was broke.

Print Henry was staring at something twisted at his feet. He pulled it into the lamplight; Taylor saw the body of a man. This man wore a blue shield-front shirt, ruined by the blood that covered his torso and was spreading down his legs and on to the earth around him. He wore a gunnysack over his head, with eyeholes cut in it.

Henry stared at Taylor dazedly. He said, 'They tried to get in. You took the gun off Charlie and killed this one. That it?'

Taylor said, 'That's it.' He found his voice was shaking, as were his arms.

Someone reached down, yanked off the hood. Henry made a choked sound; he said, 'It's Ike.' His voice was no louder than the easing groan of a rawhide hinge.

Taylor stared into the boy's face.

Henry whispered, 'Ike was a nice kid.'

Taylor said, 'That nice kid had a gunnysack over his head. He was out to lynch me.'

'What if he was? Maybe we ought to.' Henry didn't look or sound quite sane and Taylor was afraid. 'Maybe he had the right idea.'

Someone said, 'Another out here. It's Red.'

'Jesus Christ!'

'Red. Dead as mutton. Bullet ain't but an inch from the heart. Another one you killed, Taylor!'

Someone spoke in a strange, broken voice. 'Let's hang this bastard!'

Olsen asked, 'What's going on here?'

Taylor glanced at the lawman. He was surprised by the look that flickered over the man's face; what was there in that look? Guilt? Fear? Olsen stared back, he made his face calm, his lips twisted in contempt.

Print Henry squatted down. He stared at Ike, shaking his head. 'I liked Ike. I liked Red. Why'd they try a crazy thing like this?'

Olsen said, 'Well, you know kids. They go crazy; they go blind.'

Charlie Free started to rock back and forth on his rump, holding his shin. Tears glistened on his cheeks.

Henry said, 'Ike's alive! He's still alive!'

Olsen blinked. 'Still alive?'

'Bullet went in under the armpit.'

Taylor thought, Ike must have turned sideways to fire, that's how I hit him under the arm. The shot that had killed Red had been luck, not accuracy. Looking again at Ike, he felt his stomach tighten. He said, 'I'm glad he ain't dead, Henry.'

'You shut your mouth! Shut your mouth, Taylor, or I'll kill you!'

An onlooker observed, 'Most usually die, shot hrough the armpit. Both lungs shot through, usually.'

Olsen nodded, 'That's right.'

Henry scowled. 'Maybe. We can set up a bed for him. Send for the army doctor from Fort Crittenden.'

Olsen wondered, 'Why bother? He's shot through the lungs?'

Henry glared at the lawman. "Cause I liked this boy. I even liked Red, crazy as he was. They didn't do nothing we shouldn't have done, maybe. Anyway, that's it.'

Olsen shrugged, he almost looked contrite. 'All right....'

Taylor was thinking back, trying to make some sense out of this. He thought about the two boys, the red-haired boy he'd killed, the boy at his feet, shot under the armpit and through the lungs. He remembered the voices outside the door, just before the gunnysackers broke in. One of them had been the voice of an older man.

THIRTEEN

Most mornings, Arvella Shields went riding. Riding was one of the few social graces she'd learned in the East that she could employ here, even though eastern saddles were different and horses different too, another breed entirely from the small, tough, half-wild riding stock of this country. Ben had found her a fairly docile grey horse, but finding a seat for a lady to ride side-saddle was another matter; Arvella had learned to ride astride a horse.

Ben always provided an escort for her on these rides as, he told her, this was still dangerous country. This morning, her escort was the Mexican boy, Jorge. He was a handsome youth of about fifteen, so shy he was almost mute. He didn't say a word as she mounted her grey horse. Other hands idled nearby. At first she'd been flattered by the extra attentions the workmen on the ranch seemed to pay her, but then she realized why: she was a rare item, the only young Anglo woman in miles. Men came from far and wide to admire her, in the same way they might come to see a particularly notable horse or a bull of freakish colour. Not that they stood around leering – their own code of manners and fear of Ben Shields prevented that –

88

but they watched her when they thought she wasn't looking. Only Print Henry had been easy and natural in her company, from the beginning; he hadn't looked at her that way ... nor had the prisoner, Taylor.

Taylor. Why was she thinking about him? He was a man women would find attractive, if you cleaned him up ... but he'd lain with squaws, wasn't ashamed of the fact ... why should a man like Taylor have to sink down to that level?

She didn't doubt, were not Shields due to return today, that some of the hands would have taken care of Taylor themselves; left him in the brush decorating an alamo tree. Feeling about the shooting of the two boys was running high. She'd looked in on Ike herself this morning. The bloody figure under a blanket, in the squalid oven of the adobe, was somehow symbolic of this ugly world she'd chosen to inhabit. An army doctor was on his way from a nearby fort; they had to hope the boy was still alive when the medic arrived.

Arvella and the boy rode out of the ranch compound. She pointed the grey south-west today, a direction she didn't normally travel, because south-west was bad country, the beginning of a particularly mean stretch of desert. But on each of her rides recently she'd gone deeper into the back country, swung closer to the border ... and at times the urge to keep riding, the need to escape, had been almost irresistible.

They found a small tank in the hills and dismounted, resting themselves and their horses. They hadn't come so far before. She could tell Jorge was worried about this, he glanced about him nervously, kept putting his hand to his gun ... but

Arvella could have reassured him. Even Ben had to admit, sometimes, that this country was changing. Once he'd told her, 'This country won't stay like this long. It's filling up with Anglos. Soon the railroad will be through....'

Jorge told her he was going to take a little walk, his artless way of saying he was going to answer nature's call. He walked off into the brush. Arvella had a weapon, a little over-and-under derringer. She'd only fired the thing once, in practice, and she suspected it was just about useless; but she carried it anyway, as Ben instructed. Not that there was anything to fear. Ben had said, 'With the railroad, irrigation, alfalfa, a few good years, we can turn this desert into a garden.' He'd almost sounded poetic and she wondered at that. But he was right, Arizona would soon be transformed and while this transformation was taking place, there she was, married to one of the richest and most powerful men in the territory ... a man still, in part, in her thrall.

But was he? After the way things had become between them?

He believed that her coldness was part of her, that he could thaw her in time. Thinking about that, Arvella felt her lips curl in contempt. What did he know about women? His experiences were of the pay-your-dollar-roll-in-the-blanket-check-yourself-for-a-month-afterwards kind. When she thought of the other men she'd known in the East, in Europe, even Print Henry ... she could lead Shields like a child.

Ben was due to return today. Perhaps she ought to shudder at that, the heroines in the novels she read did a lot of shuddering, usually at the thought of their brutal, dominating men. Arvella wasn't the shuddering type. For all that, she was starting to wonder how much longer she could bear this ... how she hated this country! Dust everywhere, in every crease of her skin. The throat-catching stink of sweat, of horse voidings, of warm adobe and warped wood baked by the flaying sun. All colours stung, all angles were sharp and hard. Ben had hung some Virginia vines on a wall by the main ranch-house, an early, rare act of kindness before they both found out what kind of marriage this was going to be ... they were a symbol of the world she'd forsaken. But now they mocked her; they were dying, shrivelled and colourless, they'd never shoot their ruby leaves. Would she wither too, in this brutal world?

She'd been crazy for one day in her life. She'd been travelling in the East and had worked as a governess in London, Paris and Florence, and there was the offer of further work, back home, or in Europe. Then, on a vacation in New Orleans, she'd stumbled over Ben Shields' name: a rich landowner in the distant territories, advertising for a wife.

In the territories, she'd heard, life was crude and lonely. But these were only words. Arvella would marry this rich man, make her fortune and bring this country round to her terms. One of the western territories, she couldn't remember which, had become the first place in the world to give women the vote. It was a place of opportunity for a strong, determined woman.

Now she knew the desert imposed its own terms, on men and women both. She must have been mad, forsaking gentle occupation in the East for this. But her real mistake had been marrying Ben Shields. Henry, or even the squaw-lover Taylor, might take her because she was a woman they desired, but Shields just wanted a fertile womb, something to drop his sons, a brood mare to ensure his line.

Did Ben suspect Henry? Would he care?

Maybe he did, Arvella thought. Because she was surprised to find out something about how she felt … she was afraid, afraid of Ben....

Was she starting to hate her husband, boredom and indifference turning to hatred, so she could no longer stand the little things about him, let alone what she'd seen in him from the first, the brutal frontiersmam of an earlier, bloodier time, still there in a businessman's suit?

She came from her reverie, thinking where's Jorge? He'd been gone an unusually long time; had he tripped and hurt his ankle, or maybe even been bitten by a snake or a scorpion? It was unlikely but … Arvella felt a quick stirring of panic. But she wasn't helpless, like the fey creatures in her novels, who screamed and fainted at nothing. Besides, she had her horse here and she was fairly certain she could find her way back to the ranch. Still, where was Jorge?

She walked off into the chaparral, into a strange, alien world of twisted, thorn-decked plants, rock and shadow. She walked into waves of trapped smothering heat, sweat ran into her eyes, so it was a minute before she saw him, lying there. He was twisted on one side, one arm reaching out, fingers biting into the sand; his face had been pushed into the earth, sand filled his gaping mouth, he stared.... Arvella told herself, this isn't happening, this can't

be, it can't be. Jorge can't be sprawled there, mouth
wide, eyes bulging.... She'd never seen a dead
person, but he was dead ... the earth darkened by
the growing lake of blood under his chin. She
glimpsed the wound above his bandanna, the slash
across his throat, a deep, jagged grin.

She might have fainted then, like a heroine in a
novel. She might have screamed. But as she
opened her mouth she heard a stone turn
underfoot, behind her, a toe scrape gravel, very
near. As the scream started, a hand came from
behind, clamped itself about her mouth....

At dawn, Shields and his riders were in the foothills
of the Santa Ritas, twenty or so miles from the
ranch. After the briefest of breakfasts, they set off,
hoping to make the ranch before noon. The wind
had vanished, the horsemen crossing a breathless,
unshaded land of fierce heat. It was too hot for
riding, but Shields was thinking about his wife,
they'd spent too much time apart in their year of
marriage. At mid-morning they came to a tank half
full of water and emptied it. Shields reluctantly
called a halt, the riders shading up under their
horses. He picked one rider to go ahead, because
his horse was in the best shape, to another tank in
the hills that usually retained some water, giving
the man a large waterbag to fill.

He was puzzled to see this man returning after
only ten minutes. The hand dismounted and
dropped the empty waterbag at his feet. He told
Shields he'd come across the tracks of an unshod
horse. An Indian pony.

Shields said, 'Papago.'

The cowboy glared doubtfully. He'd seen the

horse's droppings; they contained grama grass.
Shields knew what that meant. Anglos fed their
horses grain, Papagos, like Mexicans, gave their
horses maize. Only wild Indians – Apaches – fed
their animals on grama grass. And where there was
one, there might be more – maybe even a war
party.

This was west of Apache country and it had been
peaceful around here for a long time, but only a
fool trusted the peace. Not with Chiricahua and
Mexican Apache renegades still hiding out across
the border.

The men caught the edge in Shields' voice as he
ordered them to mount up. Shields kicked his grey
horse into movement. He yelled at the riders to
keep their eyes skinned.

They all knew what to look for.

At the ranch, all was excitement. Henry told
Shields of the shooting last night, how a couple of
hands had tried to lynch the prisoner. One of the
gunnysackers, Red, had been killed by Taylor; the
other, Ike, was laid up in the bunkhouse and not
expected to live. Shields listened, not hearing; not
after Henry told him that Arvella had gone riding
this morning, as usual, with only one escort – the
Mexican boy, Jorge. Henry turned white when
Shields told him of the Indian sign. Shields called
for a fresh horse and swore at Henry and the
others with him until the animal was brought up.
He leapt into the saddle and broke the animal into
a run, regardless of his age and the day's heat; it
was all Henry, and others, could do to keep up with
him. The trail of Arvella and Jorge bent south and
west, towards the malpais, the bad country. Shields

and the other riders reined in, their horses lathered and blowing.

Then they saw the buzzards.

FOURTEEN

Olsen squatted in the shade of an alamo tree. Shields had planted a spaced line of these cottonwoods as a windbreak, east of the main house. The lawman took cigarette papers from his Bible. He noticed a horseman approaching through the haze; he became too intent in watching the rider and shaped the cigarette all wrong. He swore at that. He couldn't let anyone see how frightened he was.

Perhaps he should just have faded into the mesquite when the lynching went bad, but that wasn't how he worked. To win you had to take chances and he liked to win. There was a bullet with his name on it somewhere, or a stretch of desert he wouldn't make, or what the rotted-away insides of some crib-girl might leave him. Some day he'd lose the final hand, but why start losing before that? Most likely the kid, Ike, was finished; should he survive, or manage a few sentences before he died — how Olsen had set up the lynching, then deserted his companions when it all went sour — things would be different.

The red-haired boy — someone would have pulled a trigger on him eventually. He was a no-account. Olsen felt vaguely uneasy about Ike, but he hoped the boy would die soon; it might come down to the boy's neck or Olsen's and Olsen was uncommonly fond of the latter. He grinned, thinking of that.

The desert trembled under a haze of stunning heat, inverted mountains fanged a rippling, oily lake. The nearing horseman slipped from this haze. Olsen saw it was Shields, his horse staggering. He reined in and dismounted clumsily. He appeared to have lost his sombrero, his hair was awry. He half-walked, half-ran to the adobe where they kept Taylor chained. Olsen wondered why anyone would hurry in this heat.

A dog came from under a wagon, sat, scratched itself with a hind leg and panted, tongue dripping. He'd seen it slinking around the ranch before, an old, grey mongrel bitch. He reached towards it, sneering at the fear in the animal's eyes. He locked the bitch's head between his powerful hands and flipped his thumbs; he rubbed the mongrel's grey-black ears gently. He said, 'I ain't got nothin'. Sorry, dog.' The dog wagged its tail. Olsen noted how its ribs scored its flanks like wagon hubs. A hand walked past; Olsen asked him, 'Hey, why don't you ever feed that dog?'

He could see other riders approaching, more crazy men pushing their horses too hard in this heat; he thought the nearest rider might be Print Henry. He remembered Shields almost tumbling from his horse. And suddenly Olsen thought of his own father; he was fourteen, it was a quiet clearing in the Wisconsin forest and they'd been chopping wood. His pa was staring at him, saying, his voice heavy with the old country accent, 'Vot are you looking at, poy? Don't look at your father like that, or I led you have a taste of my belt.' And the old man had lifted his thick belt with its heavy brass buckle. Olsen recalled that it was only then that he saw his pa was old, old and sick, time was stooping his back, thinning arms once roped with muscle. In that instant, Olsen realized the balance had shifted between them. Pa wouldn't use his belt on his son any more, because the son was now the stronger of the two. If he wanted to, the fourteen-year-old boy could take the belt away from Pa; he might even break one of the old bastard's arms like the shanks of a bird, because he'd finally realized it could be done. That was the day he became a man, independent, his moment of release.

Olsen shaped another cigarette and this time he did a perfect job. Why had he suddenly thought back to that day, and his pa? Perhaps, for the first time, Shields looked old to him too, old, sick, used-up. A great slab of rotting beef, shoulders braced for the poleaxe.

'The knife under the armpit.' Shields unwound his bandanna, rubbed his neck. 'Throat cut, too.'

Taylor sleeved sweat from his eyes.

Shields wiped his face with his bandanna. 'Henry leave my wife go with just that little chilli-eater, Jorge. I ought to kill him for that. Some Apache renegade sneaks up, kills the Mex and takes her. The trail went south-west. They got three, four hours' start on us.'

'They? Only tracks of one Indian.'

'There ain't gonna be just one of 'em, is there? Likely there's a few more hid out. They got a three-hour start on us. You understand?'

Henry came into the adobe.

Pathetically, Shields said, 'You understand, Taylor?'

Taylor said, 'I've got to eat something.'

Henry blinked. 'What?'

In the voice of a pleading child, a voice that didn't belong to him at all, Shields said, 'Taylor, you know all about this! Minutes count....'

Taylor knew what Shields meant, but it would be impossible to prevent the woman being raped if a bunch of broncos had hold of her. Getting her back alive would be almost impossible. Taylor said, 'Shields, you put me on a horse right now, I'd fall off. I need to eat something first and drink a lot of water before I'll be fit to do anything.'

Taylor was surprised when the rancher nodded.

Taylor lifted his leg. 'And take off these goddamn irons!'

Shields nodded a second time. 'Henry!'

'Yes, boss?'

'Well, take 'em off, goddammit!'

Henry freed the prisoner from the leg irons. Taylor groaned and kneaded his ankles. Olsen entered the adobe. He put one hand to his holster gun when he saw the captive unchained.

Shields said, 'You can get her back, Taylor. I know you can. You done it before.'

Taylor had tried several times to rescue white captives from Apaches. Each time he'd failed, but he didn't tell Shields that. He said, 'I can try.'

'You're more of a white man than I figgered.'

Henry declared, 'This is 'cause Miz Shields stopped me from quirtin' the hide off you. Ain't that it, Taylor?'

Taylor glanced at the top hand with contempt.

Olsen asked, 'What is this, Shields?'

Taylor continued to rub his ankles, gasping with pain. He said, 'I tell you what else I want.'

'What?'

'I want two of your best running horses.'

'All right.'

'No saddle. Just a blanket. A good rifle and pistol. Ammunition. Plenty. Grain. A knife. Some rope. Plenty.'

'All right. What else?'

Olsen said, 'You ain't lettin' him go?'

The rancher said, 'Apaches took my wife.'

'Christ!'

'Killed a Mex kid and took her.'

'Jesus Christ!'

Shields pressed his hand to his forehead, he closed his eyes. 'You can get her back, Taylor. I got all the hands out looking, but you can get her back.'

Olsen said, 'Your crazy, Shields? You let him go, what's to stop him from running the other way?. What's a white woman to him? He prefers squaws to—'

'I want my wife back, Olsen.'

Henry said, 'Never was no real a proof he was in with the stock thieves. Only your say, Olsen.'

With sarcasm, Taylor said, 'Thanks, Henry.'

Olsen said, 'You ain't setting him loose!' He began to lift his pistol from his holster but Henry had his gun out first. He pushed the barrel of the weapon into the lawman's side, cocking the hammer. Olsen stiffened. Henry took the lawman's gun.

Olsen said, 'You can't do this, Shields. You might think you're great God almighty, but you ain't above the law!'

Shields balled his hands into fists, he closed his

eyes once more. He opened and closed his mouth. Taylor gazed at him and frowned. The rancher looked like someone losing his mind before their very eyes, something comic, tragic and frightening all at the same time. His eyes opened. 'You think I count under some two-bit county lawman? Round here, *I'm* the law.'

Olsen sneered, 'Let's see you grin, Taylor. You can grin all you like, you horsethieving bastard. This thing ain't finished yet.'

Shields closed his eyes a third time. He declared, ' *"The Lord shall smite thee with a consummation and a fever and with an inflammation and with an extreme burning and with the sword and with blasting and with mildew and they shall pursue thee until thou perisheth … and thou shall grope at noonday as the blind gropeth in darkness and thou shalt not prosper in thy ways!"* '

Taylor said, 'And I tell you what else I want.'

FIFTEEN

Next day, just after noon, Calvin Taylor reined in his horse. The animal was staggering with weariness, coat dark with sweat and dust, foam dripping from the muzzle; the rider was nearly as spent. The other horse, which Taylor led on a trailing line, was in a little better repair surprisingly, given the day's heat, the pace of the trail and the roughness of the country they'd crossed today.

Taylor dismounted. Even travelling as he'd done, changing from one horse to another, and not pushing either animal to the limit, had worn horses and rider to the bone; they'd not manage the same pace tomorrow. So Taylor's hunch had better be right, if they hoped to find Arvella Shields alive.

Scouting the scene of the kidnapping, where the sand was still faintly discoloured by the blood of the murdered Mexican boy, Taylor could only find sign of the one Apache. What if there was only one such raider? A stray travelling from his refuge in the Sierra Madres back to the reservation perhaps … and perhaps someone else. That was where Taylor's hunch came in. The only Apache he'd seen in the last few months had been the renegade scout, Choddi, in the robbers' roost. Could this man have followed Taylor all the way from the roost to the Shields' ranch, hiding himself somewhere nearby, on the lookout for who knew what? There'd been some kind of trouble over Choddi, Taylor remembered. He'd served efficiently in the Victorio campaign and then there'd been an incident on the reservation. Choddi had deserted the scout corps, he'd vanished. Taylor couldn't recall the details but he thought a woman might have been involved ... a White Mountain Apache girl who'd turned up raped and strangled. Choddi had a nickname, the other Apaches called him 'Loco' or crazy. Maybe that was because he thought you could trust the white man ... perhaps there was another, more sinister, reason....

So Taylor followed his own long hunch, that the kidnapper was the scout-turned-horsethief Choddi, who at the last minute couldn't keep his hands off an Anglo woman who put herself in his path. One thing was certain, if there was only one kidnapper, he couldn't travel far with his victim. He'd have to hide up with her, somewhere. Shields' hands were scouring possible hiding places on the ranch, or on the Papago reservation. Following his hunch, Taylor had taken the most direct route south and west towards the Canyon of The Dead. If he was right, Choddi had the girl somewhere nearby, probably in a little canyon. Knowing what a hornet's nest he'd stirred up, once he'd done with the girl he'd cut her throat, or drop a rock on her head, or finish her like he'd finished the White Mountain Apache girl. Not that the situation would be any different if Taylor's hunch were wrong and a band of broncos had her, she'd still end up the same way.

Taylor gave the horses some water then left

them chewing beans and leaves from mesquite trees. He sat on the earth, groaning and kneading cramps from his legs. He studied the broken land to the east, cactus forest and chaparral tilting up into the beginning of the mountains. He guessed he was ten or fifteen miles south of the border, midway between the Shields' ranch and the robbers' roost. He'd seen some dust earlier, about five miles to the east, enough dust for a small party of riders. Perhaps only two riders. Of course, that might mean wild Indians or smugglers or bandits or revolutionary soldiers from one faction or another, or perhaps even some of Taylor's old friends from the Canyon of The Dead. It could even mean – an unlikely scenario in this corner of northern Mexico – law-abiding citizens about some ordinary, peaceful business.

Taylor cleaned and oiled the pistol and rifle Shields had given him. The look of the country to the east reminded him of another place, high in the Sierra Anchas, where the Apaches came to dance the marriage dance. He found himself half-listening for Nah-Lin's laughter, bell-like in the dry, clear air of the high country, with plenty of echo between one mountain and the next ... but Nah-Lin was dead, and the child, Nachay. Taylor regretted he wasn't like the Apaches, who believed in ghosts, and talked to them, he couldn't find the same comfort they did in the dead.

It was working itself up into an afternoon hot enough to fry the hinges off Hell's front gate. Taylor planned to sleep in the shade, now, whilst the horses rested in the bosky, then, at dusk, he'd scout the country to the east, investigate that dust. Thinking about Nah-Lin, about what had happened to her, he felt the need for violence. He was in the right frame of mind for Arvella Shields' kidnapper.

He wormed into the shade of some smoke trees and curled up under a blanket with rifle and pistol to hand. The trailing line of one of the horses – the sorrel gelding – he laid underneath him. There was enough cover here for safety and the ground downslope was strewn with gravel and loose shale, so not even the most cat-footed Apache could cross it silently. He remembered Olsen saying, 'What's to stop him from running the other way?' Maybe he should have done just that. Why was he doing this? He turned the question over in his mind for a few minutes and whilst doing so, fell asleep.

It was a troubled sleep, full of dreams. Pa was there, no older than when Taylor saw him last, fifteen years before. Pa was shouting something, his son couldn't hear the words, but he knew what the old man would be spouting. Pa's face shifted and became Shields', which was understandable, within the logic of dreams. Shields was whining, pathetically, 'You can get her back, Taylor. I know you can,' and then he was shouting, '*And thou shall grope at noonday as the blind gropeth in darkness ... and the womb shall forget him ... the worm shall feed sweetly upon him ... he shall be no more remembeed; and wickedness shall be broken as a tree!*' Shields changed into Zachary Powers, a massive red face, upside down, the mouth saying, 'Cut the sonofabitch down,' and then Print Henry saying, 'This is an animal. Squaw lover.' Arvella Shields was there also, not the beautiful woman smiling in cool amusement at Taylor, down at Henry's feet, the

Texan raising his quirt, but Arvella Shields as she must look now.... He heard Charlie Free crying his shin was broken, tear-lines glistening on his cheeks; he saw the face of the boy, Ike, Taylor's bullet through both of his lungs, Cullen Anders slamming against him, dead weight. Heard the *charro*'s Catholic prayer over the dead man's grave and heard Jubilee crying, 'I ain't in this!' Then the crack of the rifle and Nah-Lin's laughter, knocking between the faces of the mountains and the baby, Nachay, crying in the cradleboard on her back....

The sorrel, tugging on the trailing line, woke him. He had his hand to the lever of the Winchester before he'd fully opened his eyes. To his alarm, he saw he'd overslept; it was twilight. He stared at the dark shape of the horse. The animal was looking east, ears pricked that way also.

Taylor got to his knees, studying the ground to the east. He'd planned to use the cover of early darkness to scout out his enemy, but perhaps the kidnapper had the same idea; to hide the girl somewhere, (should she still be alive) and hunt the man on his trail. And Taylor had helped by oversleeping. He wondered, for the first time, if he was getting too old for this business.

Desert twilight was brief, soon it would be full darkness. He saw himself in a black void, with unseen enemies closing in on all sides and felt chill fingers of panic on his neck and shoulders. The land around him was purple-black, the sky a fading, cindery hue. A night wind stirred foliage, so that the shadows trembled, a rippling cross-barred pattern that might conceal a dozen enemies.

Taylor rolled out from under his blanket and

wormed into the shadow pattern under the nearest smoke trees. He moved upslope. Then he halted, crouched down, keeping very still. He listened to the quick pulse of his heart, the breath caught in his throat, the thick sound of blood in his ears. If the sorrel's instincts were right, if it wasn't spooking at shadows or the scent of a wolf, then Taylor's enemy was in these same trees, moving downslope to kill his pursuer in his bedroll....

Taylor found himself wondering, once again why am I doing this? Risking his life for who? A woman who'd found pleasure in the way he'd looked, blood on his mouth, down in the dust before Print Henry. Why had she stopped Henry from using his quirt on the prisoner?

Shields had said, 'You can get her back.' The inference was plain; only Calvin Taylor could do this job. No one else but the Indian scout, the range detective, the mankiller, could get it done. Rescue a white woman from Apache renegades? Nothing but a little light exercise to the Shadow Man! Shields' desperate plea had been straight to Taylor's vanity. And he'd gone for it like the vainest fool alive.

Twilight ended but the darkness that followed wasn't absolute. There was a nearly full moon, making the woods a tangled checkerboard of silver and black, if anything, more frightening than deep and total blackness. The net of trees and tree shadow made him think of a spiders' web and he was a fly glued helplessly to the strands of the web, whilst the predator drew near.

Taylor was just about to move from his hiding place when one of the horses whickered. At the same instant, Taylor heard the snapping of a twig.

The sound came from the trees on the slope above him, and close at hand. But how close?

Taylor listened, cold with fear; he listened until he felt almost dizzy with the near-silence around him. Perhaps he was getting spooked by nothing, after all; suddenly he couldn't bear the stillness and silence any longer. He stood, took one step forward. At the same instant a man stepped from the shadows and almost walked into him.

Taylor made a gagging noise in his throat, a mixture of fear and startled surprise; the other gave a similar surprised grunt. Taylor stood face to face with an Apache.

In that first instant of meeting Taylor saw the Indian was naked to the waist, he had a Mills cartridge belt about his middle. He wore a knee-length cloth kilt and baggy moccasins. There was a red rag across his temples and a rifle in his hands. Across his cheeks and the bridge of his nose his dark face was split by a chevron of white bottom-clay, making him seem like some fierce, dark hawk.

That slash of white warpaint gave the Apache an extra second of time; it took that long for Taylor to recognize Antelope, Choddi, under the warpaint and in that second, Choddi struck.

He lashed out with the barrel of the Henry carbine. The barrel caught Taylor across the left arm, numbing it and he let his own rifle fall. The Apache began to swing the carbine around, to fire into the other man almost point blank; but Taylor sprang forward, grabbing the barrel of the Henry, forcing it down. They strained for possession of the weapon. Taylor was the stronger man; he twisted and tore Choddi from the earth, hurling the man backwards over his hip. The Indian struck against a tree, fell brokenly across the rocks on the slope. Taylor half-spun himself about, struck against a tree also, gasping as his knuckles banged wood; he dropped the carbine. Choddi got to his feet, moving slowly, hissing with the pain of his fall; he had a knife in his right hand.

Choddi lunged with the knife. Taylor dodged, felt the blade claw at his shirt. He grabbed the Indian's knifewrist in both hands. Choddi struck Taylor in the throat with his left elbow. Taylor tried to swallow but he was choking; he went to one knee, yanking Choddi towards him. Taylor came to a crouch, he lifted a knee, ramming it into the other man's groin. Choddi gasped, he stumbled forward, fell on his side. Taylor heard the knife clatter on the rocks. He lunged towards the fallen man. Choddi lifted his foot, catching Taylor in the stomach, the Anglo was pitched forward into the air. He somersaulted and struck the slope on his back. Taylor groaned and lay still; he felt he'd smashed every bone in his body He hadn't the strength to move again; but for all that, he willed himself to move, he rolled on to his left side and sat up. He saw the Apache on the slope above him, his back to him. The Indian stooped and lifted something from the earth: the Henry carbine.

Somehow Taylor forced himself to his feet. He half-sprang, half-fell forward. He lifted one knee, catching Choddi in the middle of the back; the Apache grunted and went to his knees. Taylor grabbed the carbine and yanked it towards him, trapping the Apache against him, the Henry barred across Choddi's throat. Taylor lifted one knee, rested it between the Indian's shoulders.

Choddi squirmed and writhed, one hand groped behind him, reaching for his enemy's throat, his eyes. Taylor moved his leg, driving his heel into the base of Choddi's skull, he pivoted forward, tipping his body weight on to the Indian's shoulders. The Apache made a high, gargling sound. His body thrashed on the rocks. He shouted through the blood spurting from his mouth.

Taylor let go of the carbine, the weapon had broken at the stock. He sat on the earth, wincing at his dozen new bruises, the many tiny wounds from rock and thorns. His arms trembled; a violent shaking took his whole body. He tried not to look at the dead Indian.

After what seemed a long time, he moved again. Slowly, he made his way upslope. He picked up the Winchester. It was too dark, now, to look for the woman, or scout out other enemies. He found a place downslope, in the bosky where he'd picketed the other horse and waited there for something to happen.

Nothing did.

He didn't sleep. In the early dawn he rode east up into the mountains, leading the spare horse. It was good ambush country he was climbing into, good terrain for bushwhackers and murderers, for Apaches and horsethieves. But Taylor scarcely noticed where he was going; all he could see, over and over in his mind's eye, was Choddi flopping on the sand, blood squirting from between his teeth, strangling his death-cry....

Finally, he saw something. It had been there for minutes, for the first time he saw it.

A buzzard.

It hung in the sky, about a mile north and east.

He rode towards this spot, dismounting and groundhitching the horses in the last grove of joshua trees before cover ran out and there was only a bare slope ahead of him, climbing to a ridge. He studied the angle of the slope, not liking the idea of crossing open ground. He'd already been jumped once in the last twenty-four hours. But he climbed the slope without incident and crawled on his belly to the crest of the ridge, peeping shyly beyond. He gazed into a little box canyon. For a few minutes he couldn't see through the haze of heat trapped in the canyon, and the pictures in his mind, of Choddi.... He told himself: forget that Indian, think about the White Mountain Apache girl Choddi murdered, what he might have done to Arvella Shields....

He saw, in the blind end of the canyon, two horses grazing, both animals hobbled. The woman lay nearby, Arvella Shields, she stared at the sky, seeing nothing. The fingermarks around her throat were like a necklace, a collar of purple-black jewels.

SIXTEEN

Pete Olsen lay dreaming, his mouth open; he dreamed he was a boy, in a still clearing in the Wisconsin forest. Pa was there, in the moment Olsen realized Pa was old and sick, he wouldn't take his belt to his son again because the son was now the stronger, and better, man ... Olsen jerked awake, floundering on the bed. He reached out blindly, grabbing the tent wall and a scorpion fell, wriggling, from the canvas on to his hand. Olsen flicked his wrist and flung the creature into space. He swore.

He said, 'You old bastard.'

He climbed from his bedroll, lifted the blanket, shook it. He dislodged a pattering spray of harvester ants, a number of crawling things he couldn't identify and a centipede, which fled towards the tent flap. He up-ended his boots, divesting them of more tiny creatures, dressed and stepped outside the tent.

He blinked against the glare of the early sun. He'd been dreaming of the green forests where he'd done his growing; bu this was his world now, the red desert, the blue mountains, heat and dust, cactus and mesquite.

Olsen cooked and ate a frugal breakfast.

112

There were three tents in the camp, each bearing the legend SOUTHERN PACIFIC RAILROAD on their battered canvas. Shields slumbered in the most distant. Today the Shields' hands would continue searching the ranch and the Papago reservation to the west. Olsen had another plan: he was going to trail Taylor, who'd gone south across the line into greaser country. Let Taylor find the girl. Shields was right about that; if anyone could get the girl away from a bunch of Apaches, it was someone nearly an Apache himself ... then Olsen would take the girl off *him* (allowing she was still alive, of course) and take the credit. Rescuing the woman from the savages, bringing her back out of the desert, that would show Print Henry and his kind, their eyes sneering at Olsen's splayed teeth, his scarred face. One day he might have to settle with Henry; he remembered the top hand, angling the barrel of his pistol into Olsen's back, taking his gun. No one made a fool of 'Swede' Olsen.

And Calvin Taylor. There was another one. He thought about the blow on the back of his head, the stolen bayo coyote horse, those two dead boys, Ike and Red ... one bullet, he owed Taylor that much ... and maybe somewhere on the trail today, he'd collect.

There was a story about Calvin Taylor: it was said wolves and coyotes followed him about, knowing sooner or later he'd bring them dinner. Sure enough, Taylor saw a yellow coyote, grinning down from the eastern ridge, gazing into the box canyon where Arvella Shields lay.

Taylor stood and made his way down into the little canyon. He walked up to the two horses, a lineback and a dun. Both of them were in bad shape; it looked as if the Apache had used his riflebutt on the animals. Perhaps that was why he'd jumped Jorge, to get a fresh horse; he'd grabbed the woman as an extra. Taylor said, 'Bastard.' He knelt over Arvella Shields and cut the ropes that pegged her to the earth, at the wrists and ankles. He slipped a horseblanket round the woman's body and lifted her gently and lay her on a patch of smooth sand nearby. He didn't look in her face whilst he did this.

There was a tank near the canyon wall, in the blind end of the box, a little rock pool where water running down the canyonside collected. Taylor drank a handful and filled his canteen, frowning when he saw how little water was left in the tank. He hung the canteen from a branch of one of the mesquites, to let the water cool.

Taylor glimpsed her face. Her lips were split, black; the bruises at her throat, where cruel fingers had bitten, were dark as amethysts.

On the sand nearby were some of Choddi's things: a good rifle – a Winchester .73 carbine, a full bandoleer of shells, a little derringer, a Remington .41, doubtless Arvella Shields', a pair of army field glasses, almost as good as the pair Taylor had left behind in the Canyon of the Dead.

Taylor turned the grey and dun horses loose, they weren't fit to ride anyway. He brought his own two horses into the canyon. Not that they were fit to travel either; he intended to rest them tomorrow. He himself felt almost drunk with weariness. He lay down, unafraid of wild Indians or other enemies: Shields' war party had been just one crazed man. Almost instantly, Taylor fell asleep.

He woke at dusk and drank from his canteen.

Seeing the woman watching him, he said, 'You want some?' and held out the canteen.

He could see that, though she stared at him, she wasn't seeing him, or anything here and now. Her stare focused sharply; she gaped at some picture in her head, sitting up so that the blanket slipped on to her lap. He ought to have dressed her, he supposed. Taylor said, 'You can get dressed, Mrs Shields.'

She continued to stare, at something he couldn't see. He managed to take a corner of the blanket and get it back up around her shoulders, but she didn't seem aware that he was there.

Taylor went over to an ocotillo and pulled up a few roots; you could grind them up and make a powder, a salve for bruises like the pitiful marks around Arvella Shields' throat. It was something he'd seen Nah-Lin do many times; it disturbed him that he was thinking about her as he worked, grinding the roots between two stones. What would Shields think of his young wife now, her hair like uncurried horsetail, her skin blistered with sunburn? Taylor decided he might be a little afraid of Arvella Shields; he'd spent too much time with the Apache and they feared the insane.

Looking about in the fading light, Taylor gathered together a vegetable meal – squaw cabbage, mesquite beans, prickly pear fruit. He asked, 'Do you want to eat something, Mrs Shields?' She didn't reply. He told her, 'We can't camp here.' He went on to explain why it wasn't safe, to camp in low ground, by a waterhole, trapped against canyon walls; they should fill their canteens and find a more open place, higher in the hills. She wasn't listening. She began to rock back and forth, staring, wide-eyed, into the closing darkness.

Taylor reached forward and gently took her arm.

He might have been a rattler striking. The woman jerked back, her arm barred across her face, her stare widened; but, again, she wasn't staring at him but at something else, trapped inside her mind. She stood and took one step backwards.

Taylor kept still. He didn't know what would happen if he moved; perhaps the woman would run off into the night.

She stood, the blanket caught against her body, the arm lifted across her face, her wild stare fixed on invisible terrors. He was reminded of a very small child, too young to express her fears in words; He could be hard on her, that might bring a reaction of tears and anger, a kind of purging, pull her back from the abyss she was on the edge of; but it might have the opposite effect, tip her over, put the seal on her madness.

So Taylor said, and did, nothing and eventually the girl sat down. He disregarded half a lifetime's experience and made his sleeping place in a box canyon, close to a waterhole.

He was awakened twice in the night. The first time the horses woke him, pulling on the lines, tugging at their picket pins. Taylor had a feeling a mountain lion was scouting out the waterhole but there were no developments. He saw the dark outline of the woman, sitting up, watching him. He whispered, 'Nothing to worry about. Go back to sleep.' He lay down and watched her; when she sank back in her blankets, he closed his eyes. Arms sliding around him woke him a second time. She buried her face in the left side of his chest. Her body trembled and her hair smelled of dust.

Taylor's arms went gently around her and felt the iciness of her flesh beneath his fingers. He thought, she's half-frozen! He pulled his blanket up over her. She murmured sounds he couldn't identify for a short time, then fell asleep. Taylor stared at the night sky, thinking about a woman's body resting against his, belonging there; a memory of the life he'd once had, that had been taken from him, or that he'd renounced, following the business of guns. The girl began to mumble unintelligibly, she wet his shoulders and chest with tears, without waking. Eventually, he slept.

When he awoke, in the early dawn, she was sitting up, combing her hair with her fingers. He was encouraged by this; she was no longer a thing without mind.

Taylor drank a little, nibbled squaw cabbage and went through the 'eat something', 'drink something', 'get dressed' routine. She ignored him, he might not have been there. He made an unsuccessful scout for more water. Returning to camp, he saw Arvella had dressed herself; she'd even brought her hair into some kind of order. He told her, 'You want to eat something.'

Arvella stared at nothing. He felt a quick stirring of temper. He said, 'Mrs Shields—' and reached over and gently touched her left forearm.

The strength in her slap startled him. She kicked at him and raked his cheeks with her nails. He had his hands full, pulling her wrists together then trapping her body against him so he couldn't be kicked. She screamed, three or four times. Then she began to cry and the sobbing shook her body. After a time, Taylor let go of her; she sat on the earth, hunched forward, making strangled, choking noises.

Taylor judged it safe to leave her for a while and went looking for food. He scared a bunch of jackrabbits out of some brush and shot two. He located a clump of prickly pear and cut some pads off the plants as they contained some moisture. He returned to the box canyon. Arvella Shields didn't seem to have moved, although she'd stopped crying. Taylor skinned the rabbits, put them on a spit and built a small mesquite fire under them.

The girl rocked forward from her sitting position and smacked her forehead against the sand. She clutched at the earth, squeezing fistfuls of soil until sand jetted out between her thumb and fingers. She rolled on the earth, struck at her head with her elbows, tugged at her hair.

Taylor turned the spit slowly, sucked on a prickly pear. What was happening, he supposed, was that she was beginning to remember. She'd been safe before, walled away in her dungeon of madness; now her sanity was returning, and her memories. She had things that had happened to her to accept; if she couldn't do that, she'd stay crazy.

He said, 'You want to eat something, Mrs Shields?'

She nodded. He gave her a few pads of prickly pear; she sucked mechanically. He told her to rub the ocotillo powder on her bruises. She surprised him again by obeying.

After a time, Arvella said, 'He'll kill you if he finds out what you've done.'

'Shields?'

The girl rubbed powder into her bruises. She flinched as her fingers traced the angry wealing at her throat.

Taylor said, 'I done nothing.'

The girl stared straight ahead. 'He'll kill you if he finds out what you've done.'

Taylor opened his mouth, closed it. He didn't know what to do or say next; so he did nothing. When the meat on the spit was ready, they ate silently. Arvella said nothing else until the meal was finished, when she asked Taylor, 'Everyone'll think it, won't they?'

He didn't reply.

She'd got a dab of grease on her chin, he saw, but she ignored it. She began to suck grease off her fingers, pausing to stare off into nothingness, her fingers still splayed, pointing upwards. 'The boy, Jorge ... that Indian. He killed him. That Indian....'

'Don't worry about him,' Taylor said. 'I killed *him*.'

'The Indian?'

'Dead as mutton.'

'Everyone will think it. My husband....'

'Shields?'

'I hate him! I hate him! I'm not a wife to him. I'm a brood mare! What can I do now? Where could I go? Everyone will know. Oh God, oh God ... He'll think it. I'll see it every time I look in his face. They'll all think it! Print Henry! You think it too, don't you? Only you don't care!'

She has to blame somebody, Taylor thought, and I'm here.

Arvella began to shout, 'Why should *you* care where I've been? I'm your level now! I'm like a squaw, aren't I? Do you want me now, squaw lover? They'll think I'm *your* level now! But I'm not! I didn't choose it! Not like you! You don't care how dirty they are, how filthy they are, what diseases you might catch! Or are squaws—'

Taylor said, 'Listen to me! There was only one Apache woman – that's right, *woman*, not squaw! She was all I wanted and the colour of her skin didn't mean nothin' to me. What she was, that's what mattered. Nothing you'd understand!'

The woman went to slap him and Taylor seized her wrist. She struggled against his hold, shouting, 'Don't touch me! Let go of me!'

Taylor said, 'Was I in any kind of a fix, she'd stick by me. Maybe that's what you ought to have, only it don't sound like you got it, Mrs High-and-mighty Shields!'

Arvella managed to break his hold. Taylor let her slap him a few times, she caught him an unexpectedly powerful blow that jumped tears into his eyes and he felt a little blood run from his nose. She smiled when she saw that and struck again; he grabbed her wrist. She kicked and struggled. 'Let go of me! Get your hands off me!'

He pushed her away, releasing his hold. She staggered, but didn't fall. He sleeved away some of the blood at his nose. He also managed a mirthless smile. He told her, 'We have to move.'

'Don't touch me!'

'We've got to move.'

She glared at him; after a time, Taylor realized he was glaring back. They were having a staring contest. He picked up his gear, carrying the Winchester with the aid of a crude sling he'd fashioned; he also draped himself in a bandoleer and a rope he hung one of the canteens from. He took the reins of his horse and set off north, not caring, then, whether the woman followed him or not. After a hundred yards, he halted, looking back; she was coming after him, leading her own horse. One of her slaps had split his lower lip. He tasted the salty blood there and that reminded him of how thirsty he was.

They climbed into the hills to the north, sometimes riding, sometimes leading the horses. Taylor hoped to make another seven or eight miles while it was still light but about five miles along, a wind rose. Taylor suspected there might be a blower coming, which was all they needed. A sandstorm would immobilize them, they might be trapped for a week. By the end of that time their food would be long finished and most of the waterholes filled with blown sand. They must be almost home, almost at the Arizona line and the Shields ranch, but a sandstorm would change all that. Their lives might hang on that wind, if it blew, how hard and for how long....

While there was still light Taylor found the most sheltered place he could and beat out a camp, clubbing half a dozen rattlesnakes in the process. Arvella built a mesquite fire. Taylor had made up a kind of pemmican, a mix of rabbit meat, beans and vegetables; they ate some of this, at first in silence. Then Arvella said, 'Taylor ... I'm sorry I said those things ... after everything you've done ... killing that Indian. I'm sorry about what I said ... about your wife.'

'We wasn't exactly married in church. White men ain't allowed to marry Indians, out here.'

The woman stared at her hands. 'After what you did for me ... to say those things ... it's just that everyone will think it. Won't they?'

Taylor said, 'I reckon so.'

Arvella seemed to sag, staring at the earth. Taylor was instantly ashamed of his words but said nothing. Instead, he had a look around. He thought about Nah-Lin. He could have told Arvella Shields that not all squaws had the pox, that a lot of Apache women kept themselves cleaner than most settlers' wives, that Apaches followed their religion a deal more faithfully than the so-called God-fearing Anglos who classed all Indians as Godless heathens ... but Nah-Lin and the Rat didn't need defending, not now. In his mind, he saw the two mounds in the snow, the larger one and the tiny grave where the child lay.

He returned to camp. Arvella said, 'Taylor?'

'Yes?'

'What was your woman called? Your Apache woman?'

'Why do you want to know?'

The woman didn't reply. Taylor lifted a skinbag of water, drank then passed the skinbag to Arvella. He said, 'Nah-Lin.'

'What was she like? Nah-Lin?'

'Well, she wasn't the prettiest of the girls there, but ... she was it for me, I knew straight off.'

'What happened to her?'

'There was some trouble with her people on the agency; her father figgered him and his band were gonna get blamed for something they hadn't done. He was frightened they'd get sent to Florida, that's where bad Indians get sent sometimes.'

'Would that be so terrible?'

'Lots of Indians sent there took sick and died. And not just that ... there was one got sent there came back eventually, a Chiricahua, a real wild one. Florida broke his spirit, all right.'

'How?'

Taylor shaped a cigarette. 'They penned up him

and his band in a little prison fort. But that wasn't the worst. The fort was on the coast, so the Indians could stand on the walls and look out to sea, which, of course, none of 'em had ever seen before. So these Apaches, who once had hundreds of miles to wander in, were trapped inside walls, inside a little box, on the edge of all this space, this freedom. The Chiricahua I told you about, he drew some pictures of it, on skins. Most of the pictures was of the sea, with the Indians gazing out at it. You could tell how he felt, like an eagle in a cage, staring out at the sky.'

'I hate them. The Apaches.'

'The Apaches are part of this country.'

'I hate this country, too.'

'Some do. They hate it because they can't change it. But me ... any other country would feel too small to me, now. Too small, too tame.' He flipped the remnant of his cigarette at a rock.

'You didn't tell me ... what happened to Nah-Lin.'

Taylor began to look over his rifle. 'Her father and his band ran away to the hills. They got caught in a snowstorm. Nah-Lin and the baby, they got separated from the rest, they was trapped in a canyon. I was off on scout. They was found too late.'

'A baby?'

'A boy.' Taylor paused in the checking of his rifle. 'Anyway, that was a long time go.'

Arvella stared into the fire. 'What you said ... it's true, isn't it? Everyone will think it?'

'I was only saying that to hurt you ... after what you said about Nah-Lin. But you couldn't help what you was saying.'

'Never mind that, everyone will think it, won't they?'

'I reckon so. No cure for it, less'n you move back East. It ain't right but that's how it is.'

There was a silence. He handed her the derringer. 'Keep ahold of this, 'case I missed any snakes.'

He walked out of camp, into a little gully on the north side. He urinated against a saguaro, standing with his shoulders hunched against the wind. As he buttoned up, he listened to the gale, frowning; it was shaping into a blower. He wondered at himself, running off at the mouth about an Apache pictograph that once touched him because he understood the painter's sense of exile, of loneliness. He understood what was happening to him; Avella Shields had touched his own loneliness; he'd opened himself up for the first time in years, a crazy thing to do with another man's wife, the wife of Ben Shields....

He came from his thoughts suddenly. In the darkness near at hand a horse snorted; he heard hooves rattling on stones. He froze, the Winchester held at waist level. Why hadn't he kept his ears open? Hairs stirred on the back of his neck and arms. He studied the gloom of the gully before him. An almost complete blackness. And then, in this blackness, something moved, taking shape, coming towards him....

SEVENTEEN

Pete Olsen reined in his horse. He slipped from the saddle and spent a minute examining the horse's feet. The wind picked up, flicking at him like a flap of canvas. The horse became nervous, shifting about. The wind was full of sand, as if the air swarmed with a myriad quartz-coloured insects. Behind the ridge, the wind pounded like a distant, angry sea.

He went around the near side of the horse and inspected the animal's legs and ankles. The gully was already growing dark, he needed to find a camping place whilst there was still light to see. He'd rest out this blower, then tomorrow he'd finish things, find the girl and settle Taylor.

He took one step backwards, to give the horse a complete looking over. At the same time he heard the sound of a gun being cocked; Taylor said, 'Keep still, Olsen.'

Olsen did as he was told.

Taylor said, 'Put your hands on your head.'

Again the lawman obeyed. He was thinking, how close? Left or right? Within range of his belt gun? If Olsen turned now, and fired, what were his chances? How much time before Taylor pulled the trigger? Olsen swore. Why hadn't he kept his eyes open?

The lawman found his throat was dry with fear. He said, in a rasping voice, 'You got the woman, Taylor?'

'Uh-uh.'

'Alive? Safe?'

'Uh-uh.'

'You kill them Indians?'

'Yes.'

Olsen grunted, a sound of admiration. 'All in a day's work, hey, Taylor? I guess the woman – I suppose the Indians had already....'

'Keep your hands where they are, Olsen.'

'In case you've forgotten, we're on the same side.'

'You should've remembered that when Shields had me chained up like an animal.'

There was a silence. This was the time, Olsen thought; this was the time when all you lived for became meaningless, futile. His back waited for the smashing impact of the bullet. *Do it now.* Wait and the pulling of the trigger got harder; wait and you gave your victim time to think of something, do something.

Taylor surprised him. His voice came again. 'Same side, uh? I ain't sure about that. You seem keen to have me out of the way, Olsen.'

'You figger I'm in with the horsethieves?' Keep him talking, Olsen thought, while I get a fix on his voice. How far away? Left or right?

Taylor said, 'That's right.'

'You're the one tied in with 'em. How come that greaser got free?'

'Those kids that tried to lynch me. There was an older man with 'em. That was you, Olsen.'

'Me? You're crazy.'

'You talked those two poor bastards into it. 'Course, you didn't run when it went wrong. You got nerve, I'll say that for you.'

'Those kids did what they did themselves.'

'You're a goddamn liar, Olsen. You got those kids killed. Question is, why? Was you just sore at me? 'Cause of your horse, 'cause of that crack on your head. Or was you in with the horsethieves, is that why you did it?'

Olsen said, 'You killed them two—' and fell on his side. He heard Taylor's rifle crack, Olsen rolled, pulling his pistol from his holster. He glimpsed a dim shape in the shadows, behind the blown dust, like a silhouette on canvas; Taylor crouching, bringing his rifle down for the next shot. Olsen lifted his pistol. They fired together.

Taylor spun, went down.

The lawman sprang to his feet, ran towards his horse. He felt almost crazy with fear. All at once the wind was crashing into him, dust filled his mouth and eyes; he saw his horse whirling around, about to run. Olsen tripped and fell sprawling. He saw the horse had got its forefeet tangled in the lines; he pushed himself to his feet and grabbed the animal's bridle. He glimpsed movement in the dust behind him, lifted his pistol and fired blindly. His nerves were suddenly all shot to hell, he realized. He vaulted into the saddle, almost bringing the horse to its knees and spun the mount about. He rode over the ridge; cresting the ridge, his back felt a mile wide. He waited for Taylor's bullet to knock him from the saddle. But no shot came. Olsen thought, maybe I killed the sonofabitch.

Riding down the far slope, he saw the Shields

woman. She was trying to hang on to the trailing
lines of a crazed horse that had pulled its picket pin
and was about to bolt. He rode up to her, grabbed
the horse's reins. She stared at him, her face
blotted out and then reappearing behind her hair.
Olsen shouted above the wind, 'We got to get out of
here, Mrs Shields!'

She shouted something, it sounded like, 'Where's
Taylor?'

Olsen glanced over his shulder. 'Back there!
Come on!'

She surprised him by obeyng; she didn't so much
as ask why, but climbed aboard the horse. He rode
out of camp and she followed.

It was a wild ride, through blown dust that hid
the surrounding world, but at least the wind was
mostly to their backs. There was a brief respite
when they got into a little high-walled canyon and
Olsen looked for a place to hole up. They dug
themselves half into the sand and buried themselves under horsegear as the wind built up again,
and raged all night.

In the dawn the wind suddenly fell, leaving
nothing but a little breeze, like a puppy shyly
licking your hands and face. The near-silence,
after the thunder-boom of the gale, popped and
crackled in Olsen's ears. He scavenged a frugal
breakfast for himself and the girl, rubbed down the
horses, fed and watered them as best he could. He
looked around for watersign. The country looked
vaguely familiar to him and he suspected they were
now on American soil, on the Shields ranch in fact,
near to where they'd captured Taylor....

Thinking about the range detective, Olsen
instinctively glanced over his left shoulder. Was the

mankiller still on their trail? Or had Olsen done for him? The fear was still in the lawman's belly, his feeling was that you couldn't get rid of the squaw-lover so easily. If he was right about where they were now, he knew the quickest way from here back to the Shields ranch. Then *he'd* be the hero, the one who brought the girl out of the desert. What will you say about that, Print Henry? What would you say about that, Pa?

Olsen told the woman, 'We'd better go, Mrs Shields.'

'We've got to look for Taylor.'

'He can look after hisself,' Olsen sneered. 'He's lived with Apaches, he ain't like a white man.'

'But if he's left out there, afoot....'

She was staring at him, alarm in her eyes; Olsen tried not to grin. She saw that and her expression changed, for an instant there was a look on her face that was almost guilty. Maybe, the lawman thought, she hadn't wanted to be rescued; maybe she and Taylor were all set to go at it, or had been going at it already, when Olsen had busted in. It wouldn't bother Taylor that she'd been the plaything of some greasy red bucks.

Olsen said, 'He'll be all right. Best thing is to get you safe back to your husband, then we can send men out to look for Taylor.'

She tried to look indifferent and Olsen tried not to smile. She nodded.

They moved out of camp, leading their horses awhile before they mounted. Olsen let the woman get ahead of him at one stage. He let his eye run along her figure, he enjoyed the way she rode. She was still something he could think about in that way, despite everything she'd been through. They didn't talk; maybe most of the time she didn't talk to the help, not even to a man who had brought her out of the desert. In his head, he saw Taylor and Arvella Shields together. If only Ben Shields found out; that was another thought that made Olsen grin. Women might go for Taylor, Olsen supposed, not just because he was a handsome man, but because he had the arrogance, the cold authority all killers had. Women always went for that kind. Olsen had the same kind of authority he knew, but his fierce ugliness put women off, he had to pay for his. But they were all whores, all women from his mother down, who'd never taken his side, who'd stood by when pa took his meanness out on his son, when the old bastard reached for his workbelt with its heavy brass buckle....

Olsen studied the land to the east, where a faint line of timber marked a wash. Beyond the trees he made out some grey-white smudges.

He glanced again at Arvella Shields. In his mind's eye he saw Taylor with her, then an Apache bronco, then Olsen ... the lawman leered at his fantasies. Not that it would ever happen. He paid for his women but drew the line at bitches who'd been with red savages, you never knew what you might catch off them. He lifted a pair of field glasses from his saddle-bags, reined in his horse and spent a minute scanning the country to the east. He inspected the grey smudges, confirming what he'd thought. They were tents.

He called to Arvella, 'Hey, girl! We're home!'

Olsen and Taylor had fired together.

Taylor felt a blow on his left side, just above the hip. The next thing he knew he was down on his hands and knees, hanging on to the world as it threatened to wrestle away from him, the wind filling his ears with a thousand tortured voices. There was no pain but a sick-making feeling of shock, of impact that had knocked all the strength out of him. Then he felt pain, a stinging on his left side. Which meant a nick. There was a rule of thumb with bullet wounds: the more pain, the less serious the injury, because a major wound would cripple the nervous system. Then Taylor felt dampness on his back, soaking his shirt through. This time it seemed the rule was wrong; he'd been seriously hit.

He thought, the first time in years I talk too much and it's killed me.

He raised his head and looked for Olsen through the wind, the screaming curtain of driven sand. He stood shakily, lifting the Winchester, surprised he could still stand, hurt as he was. If only he could spot Olsen, at least he could take the horsethieving bastard with him.

He staggered forward, taking invisible punches from the wind. A gust captured his sombrero, skimmed it away. A shot cracked through the din. Taylor sprang backwards, he landed on a slope of sand that promptly caved away. He fell. He bounced down and down. He rolled, curling into himself as sand-waves heaved over him. All the fiends shrieked in his ears. He squirmed into cover, cowered down, buried his head in his arms.

When dawn came, he was still alive, which surprised him; he was half-buried under a rock overhang like a hibernating animal. Only a little, furtive wind quested about. The lack of noise hurt his ears. He felt dried blood caked to his back. He thought, why ain't I dead?

He peeled off his shirt and the mystery was explained. One of Olsen's shots had pierced a saguaro. The giant cactus stored a lot of moisture in its body; punctured it squirted jets of liquid. There had been a saguaro right behind Taylor, a good squirt had soaked the back of his shirt. The bullet that *had* struck him had clipped his left hip bone and burned his flesh, breaking the skin but doing little damage.

He said, 'And I thought that sonofabitch Olsen had killed me!'

He laughed shakily, a weak, not-quite-sane laugh.

He went back to camp. The woman, the horses were gone; gone with Olsen, he supposed. But Taylor found the bag of pemmican and breakfasted a little better than might have been the case otherwise. He felt light-headed, not just with fatigue, thirst and the shock of his wound, but in the realization that he wasn't dead after all.

Because he was hatless, Taylor tied his bandanna around his head like a pirate – or an Apache. He decided to move north into higher ground, there might be waterholes up there not filled in with sand from last night's blower.

He found the tracks of an unshod horse. He guessed the rider was a Papago, he must be close to the Arizona line and both the Shields ranch and the Papago reservation. There was an old score between him and the Papagos, a personal thing, but they wouldn't know that; Papagos were friendly to Anglos and sided with them against a common enemy, the Apache ... so Taylor followed the pony trail and located a tank with a little water in it. He supposed he might be twenty miles from the Shields ranch house, nothing but a short hike to an Apache, but a long haul for a white man afoot ... except Taylor knew he was equal to it.

He tied the Winchester across his shoulders and draped himself in pemmican bag, ammunition belt and canteen. He began to jog northwards. He thought about Olsen as he ran, this thing between them would get itself resolved the very next time they met. He smiled grimly at the thought of that.

Towards noon, when he was looking for a place to shade up and rest out the worst of the day's heat, he heard guns. Two pistol shots, then two more. A good distance away.

A little fear tightened in his belly. Someone firing signal shots, or was there a more sinister reason? Nonetheless he set off to the north-east, moving into more broken country, climbing towards the place where the guns had sounded.

EIGHTEEN

Olsen and Arvella Shields reined in their tired horses. A steep-banked wash slashed the plain before them. A ripple of brown water moved along the bottom, enough to cover a bather's feet and ankles perhaps, wide enough to cross in half a dozen strides. Nonetheless, the riders stared at the water as if fascinated. They were only dimly aware of the camp north of the wash, behind a screen of smoke trees and cottonwoods. There were a couple of tents there, grey canvas bleached white in the sun. Olsen saw two men standing by the nearest tent and noticed that both seemed unusually tall. One of these fgures ducked back into the tent, the other began to walk towards the wash. There were some horses in a rope corral and two other men there.

The riders dismounted. They let their horses drink and then hauled them back from the wash, tying them to some trees. The girl drank and knelt in the creek, splashing water on to her face. She seemed to be trying to cry, without success. Olsen filled his canteen, then drank. He yanked off his boots and sank his aching feet into his stream, which came to his ankles.

The man coming towards them broke into a

stumbling run. Olsen recognized Ben Shields. Olsen watched in amusement, waiting for the man to take the girl in his arms. But that didn't happen. He slowed his run and halted a few paces short of his wife. He stared; he made a strangled sound in his throat. Arvella stared back then suddenly moved forward, slipping past him. Shields made a clumsy attempt to take her arm, but she avoided him; she strode through the trees. He followed, like a man walking to meet the hangman.

Olsen grinned, enjoying the scene. Perhaps a question had showed in Shields' face, the same question that Arvella Shields would always see, now, out on this frontier. No escape from it, unless she went back East where no one might know what had happened. Olsen supposed, if he was a sentimental man, he might feel pity for both husband and wife. As he wasn't, he didn't; pity didn't belong in this world.

After a time, Shields re-emerged from the trees, he approached the man sitting in the wash. Olsen didn't attempt to get up and he didn't take the mocking smile from his lips. Shields saw that, probably guessed that he was the thing being mocked. Dislike showed in his eyes, but he said, 'I don't know how to thank you, Olsen.'

'Don't thank me. It was Taylor got her back, who took care of the Indians.'

'Where's Taylor now?'

Olsen glanced over his left shoulder. 'Back there aways.'

Shields stared off at the country to the south. Olsen was expecting the rancher to ask another, obvious question but he didn't. He said, 'The Indians....' There was another question he wanted to ask, Olsen could see, but for the answer to that, he'd have to ask Arvella. The rancher said, 'Still, I'm beholden, Olsen.'

The old man looked dazed, helpless. Olsen almost felt a little pity for him after all. The big man turned and walked away. Olsen stood; he climbed out of the north side of the wash and walked into the shade of some oak trees. He sat in the grama grass and fashioned a smoke.

He could see some of a band of horses moving in the rope corral. He saw the two men there were soldiers in the uniforms of the US Cavalry. A corporal and a private. The private walked towards him. A thin man with a scanty beard and a moustache. He took off his campaign hat and revealed mousy, thinning hair. He smiled, showing buck teeth. He had narrow-set eyes. They were peculiarly vacant eyes, Olsen thought, in a face you couldn't trust or like, the rabbity nose, the small mouth crowded with splayed teeth. Olsen smiled, he was pleased to see faces as unlikable as his own.

The private asked, 'Any tobacco to spare?' His accent made him an Irishman.

'Sorry Mick.'

The man blinked. 'You see any wild Indians out there?'

'A big war party coming right this way.'

The soldier glared. 'You got a big mouth, mister.' He turned and walked back towards the corral.

Olsen called after him, 'We took care of the Indians, soldier boy! As usual, without the help of the US goddamn Cavalry! Useless goddamn buttermilks!'

Olsen smoked his cigarette. He thought about

Calvin Taylor. You could rely on most wounded men caught out in a desert blower to perish with the minimum of fuss, but not Taylor. You had to make sure of his kind. His only art was survival. Olsen would get a spare horse and supplies and return to the trail. Finish this. Just as soon as he eased the aches out of his back, legs and rump.

The corporal came from the corral, leading two horses, a grey and a dun. He began to curry the grey below the knees. Olsen forgot his trail aches and climbed stiffly to his feet. He walked over to the corporal. The soldier was squatting down, a cigarette in his mouth, his eyes slitted as if in pain or concentration.

Olsen asked, 'Where you from, soldier?'

The soldier didn't look up as he answered, 'Fort Huachuca.'

'One of Colonel Martin's yellowlegs, huh?'

'Uh-uh.'

'You got horses to sell?'

'No.'

Olsen glanced over at the dun, 'What about this one? Good horse.'

'Sure is. My horse, though.'

'I need another horse. I got money.'

'Then you'll have to need. Ain't for sale.'

Olsen let argument play on his face, then he shrugged lightly. He saw Shields emerge from the tent where he'd left his wife. Olsen walked to the rancher's side. He said, 'Them soldiers—' He nodded towards the corral.

'What about 'em?'

'See that horse? The dun? The corporal there says it's his horse.'

'So?'

Olsen sauntered around the corner of the tent. He cupped hands around the cigarette in his mouth, lit the smoke. 'It just happens to be my horse.'

'What?'

'That bayo coyote horse. It got stoled off me.'

Shields gave him a confused look. Olsen was tempted to smirk at that but didn't. The rancher said, 'Maybe the horsethieves sold them to the army legit.'

'Maybe. But I asked the corporal about his commanding officer at Fort Huachuca. Colonel Martin. He didn't say nothin' about it.'

'Why should he?'

'When I was last at Huachuca, a month ago, there was no Colonel Martin there. I'd've been surprised if there was, as I just made him up.'

'Well, what do you think? Those soldiers is deserters? Horsethieves?'

Olsen lifted his pistol from its holster and checked it over. He told Shields, 'I dunno. I aim to go ask.'

Shields ducked into the tent his wife was in. He told her, 'There might be some trouble.' She stared. He went on, 'Stay in here. If you hear shooting, lie flat.'

Olsen climbed back into the saddle. He groaned; he felt a thousand years old and his rump complained at the black collar saddle leather. For the first time he wondered if he might be getting too old for this business. The next time I get off a horse, he told himself, I'm going to stay off a good long while. Soon as this business is sorted out.

His horse was gazing longingly towards water but Olsen turned the animal's head about and rode to the corral. The corporal worked on the grey's near-front hoof with a hoof pick. He'd slipped his hat behind his head, Olsen saw there was a filthy rag banding his temples. Olsen understood the slitted eyes, the teeth ground together round the cigarette.

Olsen halted his horse just by touching the rein. The corporal was half a dozen paces ahead of him, the private twice as far away and to the left. Olsen leaned on the saddle horn, his right arm folded and hidden behind his left and his right hand settled gently on the butt of his pistol. Inside him there seemed to be a wire running from his neck through his stomach to the back of his knees, a humming, twanging wire. He felt sweat on the palms of his hands, behind his ears.

He said, 'Hey, Corporal.'

The man didn't look up.

Olsen asked, 'That horse – the bayo coyote. How long you had him?'

'Six months. Why're you asking?'

It wasn't the sort of question you usually asked out here, Olsen knew. The private was listening; he was crouched down, brushing out the near leg of a horse, holding the animal's tail at the hock. He stopped his work, stood, pretended to study the back of his hands.

The corporal also paused in his work, he straightened up. He dawdled the hoof pick in his left hand. He dropped the hoof pick and scratched his belly; his fingers worked across to his right side, hunting a crawler in his dirty blue shirt. And taking his hand close to the grip of the pistol backwards in the holster on his right hip.

This quick-on-the-trigger stuff was a product of

dime novels, Olsen knew. Speed wasn't what counted, it was being accurate and, more than that, it was having what it took to pull a trigger on another human being. The wire inside him was thrumming, pulling tight. He heard movement behind him. That would be Shields. Olsen gazed at the corporal, smiling a very little, keeping the private in the corner of his eye. He'd let Shields take the private. He'd take the non-com. Olsen knew exactly where his hand ought to be pointing when he fired, lined midway between the second and third button down on the corporal's five-button shirt....

Olsen said, 'Six months? Now that's funny—' and catapulted forward. His face rammed the horse's mane. He flopped against the animal's neck like a feedsack; the horse broke into a run. Olsen lost one stirrup, he snaked one arm about the horse's neck and knew an instant of pain so terrible it seemed to tear his chest wide open. The horse veered into the trees, one branch whipped across his forehead leaving a stripe of blood. They broke into the open, behind him were yells, running hooves, a pistol shot; he wondered what the hell was happening. He was vaguely aware that the horse was running into more timber. Suddenly the animal spun, rearing on the lip of the wash. As he bucketed about in the saddle Olsen felt very tired, he told himself, the next time I get off a horse I'm going to stay off a good long time. He leaned on the buttplate of the Remington repeater in his saddle scabbard and sagged forward. The saddle scabbard pivoted beneath his weight and he felt himself toppling. He wondered at the dampness on the back of his shirt and the pain jolting through his arms. The Remington slid from the scabbard and fell into the wash. Wearily and reluctantly, Olsen slid after it, head first, he felt his foot come out of the stirrup.

Sometime later, Olsen became aware of where he was; halfway down the bank of the wash, upside down. He lifted his eyes and saw the Remington wedged against the bank. It hurt his eyes to look at it, because the last time he'd cleaned the gun he'd overburnished the faceplate, it made a bar of blinding metal.

A horseman reined in at the top of the wash and Olsen saw it was the corporal. He was having trouble controlling his mount, which threatened to pitch him into the wash. The soldier managed to hold the horse still; he lifted his pistol. Olsen stared dispassionately at the weapon as it swung towards him. He felt the impact of the bullet and was slammed back against the earth. He began to fall. He found himself rolling downhill, through gauzy waves of dust; he heard the pistol crack again, but felt no further impact. He seemed to fall a long time. and then he was still. Wedged at the bottom of the wash, his mouth full of sand, his brain still turning as his heart still pounded. He could still hear, too. He heard a voice shouting; Shields' voice. The rancher was yelling, 'All right! Quit shooting! He's dead already! You think I ain't gonna kill a man at that range? Guess who's walking this way, right now? Afoot, coming this way?'

Olsen heard another voice, the corporal's. The soldier asked, 'Who?'

NINETEEN

Calvin Taylor squatted in the shade of a palo verde tree. He chewed mesquite beans. He looked to the north where there was a wash lined with smoke trees, and tents beyond the wash. A horseman rode out of this camp and came towards Taylor.

Taylor wondered if any part of him didn't ache. He touched the bullet burn on his left side and winced. He rested the Winchester across his lap.

The horseman halted his horse fifty paces or so from the range detective. He called, 'Taylor, you all right?'

'Shields.'

'I figgered Olsen might've killed you. We got Arvella. Olsen brung her in.'

'Where is Olsen?'

'Hid out. I dunno where.'

'Who are them soldiers?'

'Cavalrymen from Fort Huachuca. Despatch riders. They took shelter with us from the blower. I suppose you was caught out in that.' Shields lifted his hat – a needle-crowned sombrero – from his head a moment, wiped sweat off his forehead with the back of his forearm. He said, 'Listen, Taylor. It's all right. We can rub out all that old talk.'

'What? About me being a horsethief?'

142

'That's right.'

'How many days you had me chained to the floor, like an animal? For no good reason. Except Olsen's say-so.'

'I know. I figgered we could rub all that out.'

'Having to sit and smell my own dirt bucket.'

Shields mopped more sweat from his face with a bandanna. 'I figgered we could rub all that out. What do you want, an apology? I apologize.' There was a pause, then Shields said, 'You look all in, man. We got food in camp.'

'All right.'

Shields rode slowly back to camp, Taylor walked after him. When he reached the creek he knelt and drank earthy water. The sun was sucking the wash dry. Taylor stood; he saw Shields emerge from his tent and stride towards the creek. Taylor thought he glimpsed another man at the tent flap but he might have been mistaken, he was a little sun-dazzled. As the rancher approached Taylor said, 'I heard some shots.'

'One of them soldiers shot a snake. Here, man.' Shields offered his canteen. 'We got the food going. We'll find you a hat, too.'

The range detective glared at the older man.

Shields said, 'You got my wife back, Taylor.'

Taylor drank from the canteen. He watched a pair of buzzards. They cut tightening circles, marking a place 200 yards north-east, where the wash dog-legged. Shields followed his gaze. The rancher said, 'Something dead out there.'

'Not yet. They'd be spiralling down if it was.'

The two men climbed the north bank of the wash. At the top, Taylor stumbled. He would have toppled backwards if Shields hadn't caught his sleeve and held him.

'Thanks, Shields,' Taylor said. To his surprise, the words cleared his throat without difficulty. As Taylor stepped past Shields, the rancher drew his pistol from his holster and struck the range detective above the right elbow. He knocked the man down. Shields threw Taylor's Winchester back into the wash and jammed the muzzle of his pistol against the nape of Taylor's neck. He grinned and said, 'I guess I'm a liar, Taylor.'

The other man pushed himself to all fours, got to one knee. He rubbed his arm. He felt almost dead with weariness and dehydration but there was no time for that, he needed to be clear-headed, he needed all his strength now. 'Listen, Shields. If you still think I'm in with those stock thieves, you're wrong. I figger Olsen's your man.'

'Olsen?'

'You had him and you let him slip through your fingers.'

'I got all the horsethieves I need right here.'

'Listen, Shields,' Taylor said, in a reasonable voice. 'Listen you ungrateful old bastard, unless your hearing is as wore out as anything else....'

'You've got a mouth on you, all right, just like Olsen said.'

'I told you, Olsen—'

He was conscious of another man approaching. This man said, 'We took care of Olsen.' His accent made him a Texan. Taylor squinted against sun glare and recognized Griffin, still in the uniform of a corporal of cavalry. He'd pushed his hat back on his head so Taylor saw a filthy bandage across his forehead. The deserter cradled his Springfield Long Tom in his arms. He said, 'Now ain't this a nice surprise?'

'I'm sure it isn't,' said Zachary Powers as he lifted the flap of Shields' tent and stepped out into the sunlight. He was wearing what appeared to be a pith helmet of some white material and the same black broadcloth suit he wore at the robbers' roost. Then, as now, sweat squeezed out of his red flesh, he mopped at it with a bandanna already soaked through.

The other soldier came into view, a man in the uniform of a private. He had a narrow, rabbity face and splayed teeth. He declared, 'So this is the great Calvin Taylor.' His accent made him an Irishman.

The corporal observed, 'He don't look much now, does he?'

Taylor said, 'I should've made sure of you when I had the chance, Griffin.'

The Texan sneered but couldn't keep a hint of anger from his eyes. 'Careless of you.'

'I'll remember next time.'

Powers smirked. 'Next time, Mister Taylor? You're an incurable optimist.'

Taylor stood. He flexed the fingers of his right hand, making sure they did what he wanted them to do. He saw a bulge in the vest pocket of Powers' waistcoat – any kind of pocket gun. There was a Remington-Rider-sized bulge in one of the pockets of his frock coat. The soldiers had belt guns, in addition to Griffin's Long Tom. The rancher kept his pistol trained on the area of Taylor's belly.

Taylor was thinking, where's the girl? In one of these tents? Was she just going to sit there while they did this, to the man who'd brought her alive out of the desert?

Griffin said, 'Let's get it over with.'

Powers took his bandanna and mopped at his neck. 'Not yet. Mr Taylor deserves some kind of explanation, don't you think? We can't let him die in ignorance.'

The corporal walked over to the corral. The private drew his Army Colt, seemed to be checking the sighting of the barrel. Powers sat on a rock in the shade of the smoketrees and filled his pipe. He took a long drink from a canteen, afterwards wiping his lips with the back of his wrist. Seeing him drink, Taylor felt thirst like fire in his throat; he tried to judge how weak and tired he was, whether he had the strength for what he had to do.

Powers smiled, the pipestem between his teeth. 'You shouldn't be so surprised, Mr Taylor. Didn't I tell you that I sold stock on both sides of the line? Mr Shields and I are, if not exactly partners, close business associates. Obviously, if stock pilfering is endemic, his herds must be pilfered too, or else questions would be asked. Occasionally we have to sacrifice some of our fraternity, again for appearance's sake. But the deficit is made up, I assure you. We have a very tidy little business.'

'Very tidy.'

'Of course, we can't maintain this front indefinitely. So many people have to be kept in ignorance.'

Shields said, 'Like Print Henry. He ain't in on this. I bet you figgered he was, didn't you Taylor?'

Griffin came back from the corral. He held a coil of rope in one hand. Taylor stared at the rope, he couldn't help it. He thought, do they hang me? Or drag me behind a horse? Dragging was a cruel sport the Anglos had learned from the Apaches, who had themselves learned it from the descendants of Spanish conquistadores. Hanging was as bad, though. Out here it was called strangling, with good reason; it was an easy job to botch. The *charro*, Augustin Jarocha, had said, 'Better a bullet than a rope'. Had the *rurales* granted his wish? He was right, Taylor decided; a bullet was better.

Powers trickled a very little water on to his kerchief, rubbing the damp part of the cloth into his face and neck. He said, 'Neither was, what'shisname, Olsen? We had great hopes he might join us. After all, what kind of money does a country policeman earn? But you were quite wrong about him, Mr Taylor. Olsen turned out to be – after his own peculiar fashion – that rarity, an honest lawman. Most regrettable to all concerned. Particularly to him.' Powers gazed off into the distance, where the buzzards hung in the sky.

Shields glanced at the pistol in his hand, as if he'd only just remembered it was there. He slipped it back into his holster. That only left the private with a drawn weapon in his hand.

Taylor said, 'What about that Indian, Choddi?'

Powers pulled off his necktie. 'I control things in the robbers' roost. But it has to be a tenuous sort of control. New parties drift in and out very often. I don't inform them of all the intricacies of the situation. I feel that is best. Also, often, there's a language problem. Choddi knew nothing of my arrangements with Mr Shields here. Even if he had – well, that Indian was always a little touched. I don't condone what he did, Mr Taylor, quite the opposite. He would have found that out, had he returned to the roost. But you concluded that matter most satisfactorily.'

148 *Canyon of the Dead*

Griffin declared, 'Made a good Indian out of him.'

Shields gave the prisoner a troubled look. 'I have to thank you for that, Taylor.'

Taylor told the rancher what he could do with his thanks.

Shields flushed. He declared, ' *"The wicked is snared by the transgression of his lips ... a man shall eat good by the food of his mouth, but the soul of a transgressor shall eat violence. He that keepeth his mouth—"* '

Taylor said, ' *"... Keepeth his life; but he that openeth wide his lips shall have destruction! Judgements are prepared for sinners, and stripes for the backs of fools!"* '

Shields blinked.

Taylor said, 'My pa was a preacher. A big, empty, dirty-thinking bag of wind like you. Main reason I left home. Got sick of goddamn breakfast-table sermons.'

The girl came from the tent, halted and stared at the group of men. Shields turned towards her, shouting, 'Arvella! Get back in the tent!'

'What are you doing?'

Shields breathed slowly through his nostrils. 'Mr Taylor and I are ... settling some things.'

She ought to protest now, ask questions; Taylor waited for that. She ought, at least, to look him in the face. Instead, she nodded slowly.

Shields voice caught when he said, 'Get back to your tent!'

Again she nodded and turned away.

Taylor opened his mouth; he was going to call her name, the hell with what Shields thought; what difference would it make now anyway? The private

was staring at her, nothing guarded about the look
on his face, his smile became a leer. Shields saw that
and his face coloured. In the same instant the
woman swung back towards them, she'd worked
the little derringer from her sleeve, her thumb at
the hammer of the tiny gun.

Taylor sprang. His elbow caught the private in
the chest. The soldier went down with a grunt, dust
bloomed around him. He dropped his pistol.
Taylor grabbed for it. Griffin lunged at him but
Powers got in the way. Taylor almost had his
fingers to the grip of the pistol when Griffin kicked
it along the earth. He leapt at Taylor; Taylor
folded sideways; Griffin tripped over him and fell
headlong. Rising, Taylor kicked the corporal in the
back.

He heard the snap of the derringer. The private
had snatched up his gun, he swore and stepped
back one pace. He dropped the pistol once again,
sat on his rump. He touched his side, lifted his
hand, stared at the blood on his fingers and gave a
small, incredulous laugh.

Shields seemed undecided between grabbing his
wife and tackling the prisoner; he came towards
the latter. He started to pull his holster gun when
Taylor hit the man on the point of the chin. Shields
went back on his rump. Falling, he struck against
Arvella, who staggered; Powers grabbed her wrist,
wrestled with her for ownership of the derringer.
She kicked at him, one kick finding his groin. The
heavy man gasped but kept his hold.

Griffin was on his feet; he came at Taylor who
caught him with a right cross, knocking him back
on one knee. The private was also on his feet, he
caught Taylor with a wild punch to the chin.

Taylor punched in return. Then Powers stepped in and knocked Taylor down. It was a poleaxing blow to the right cheek. Taylor writhed about a minute, getting stars and bright lights out of his vision. In the same minute Griffin sprang on to his back and pinned him face down to the earth. Taylor was aware that Shields had lifted Arvella, was carrying her, as she kicked and yelled and fought, back to the tent. Taylor tried to rise; the private began to kick at his head.

'That'll do!' Powers cried. 'We aren't goddamn animals!'

'This here's the animal,' Griffin said, half-panting.

'If so, a superb animal,' Powers conceded. 'In terms of resourcefulness, physical prowess, fortitude. Although emotionally an infant, of course.'

Shields returned from his tent. He seemed to be using both hands to adjust his jaw. He said, 'Let's get on with it!'

The private winced and rested his hand against his side. 'Your woman shot me, Shields!'

Griffin gave the other deserter a contemptuous glance. 'Only a burn. You ain't gonna die.'

'I'll settle that crazy bitch.'

Shields glared. 'I'll settle you, and now, you talk about my wife like that!'

Powers' punch had ripped open Taylor's right cheek; his face felt stiff with blood and the wound pulsed fiercely. He had to squint to see properly. He told the rancher, 'She ain't your wife no more, Shields! That's your marriage done for!'

Shields blinked. He said, 'Fetch up a horse.'

Griffin used a length of rope to tie Taylor's hands before him. 'No horse for this sonofabitch.

He's too fly.'

The Texan studied one smoketree that nature could have designed for a hanging. It was squat and thick bodied, one great bough arched from the trunk. Taylor watched in sick fascination as Griffin fashioned a noose from the rope he held. He made a good job of it.

The private asked, 'What's he gonna stand on?'

The corporal grinned. 'Nothing! We just hoist him straight up!'

'Jesus! Hoist him!'

'I saw it done once, to a miner in Gunsight.'

Powers said something which Taylor didn't understand. 'Civilization has come around you like a noose, Mr Taylor.' He studied the grazed knuckles of his right hand.

Shields said, 'I knew you'd finish up with a noose around your neck, Taylor, first time I laid eyes on you. Some men are just born to hang.'

'Somethin' you ought to remember.'

'Me? You're way off, Taylor. I got big things in store. Arizona's getting a railroad. What with the Indians all pacified, it'll be a state soon. Me'n Powers'll be big actors in this country then.'

Griffin asked, 'You got the woman tied in her tent? She shouldn't see this. Bad business, hanging. Your face goes all purple and your tongue sticks right out, turns black. You piss down your leg. Sometimes it takes you fifteen, twenty minutes to strangle properly.'

Taylor said, 'Something *you* ought to remember.'

The Texan smiled at that. He threw the rope into the air, played it over the bough of the smoketree. The noose hung, a deadly pendant.

Shields was sweating badly. 'I take no pleasure in

this! Let's get it done!'

Powers brushed dust from his frock coat. 'There's still something else that needs saying.'

TWENTY

Just another three yards, you son of a bitch.

Olsen told himself, *you can do it.* After what he'd already done, he could make three more yards.

How many could have done that? Climbed up out of the wash, carrying a heavy rifle, all the time with two bullets through him, Well, Pa, what do you say about that? Ugly Pete Olsen, the scar-faced Swede lawman, the man killer, who got the two boys, Ike and Red, killed, he'd done that ... and he wasn't finished yet.

One bullet wound wasn't much. The corporal's shot had gone under the flesh, skated over his lower left-side ribs and exited an inch above his left hip. But the other bullet was another story; it had angled through his back doing God-knew how much damage and punched out of his guts, leaving an exit hole he could bury his fist in.

It must have been Shields who backshot him. Why? Olsen must've been all wrong about this business, about it being Taylor's doings. Maybe the range detective had let the *charro* get loose just so he could follow him, trail him back to the robbers' roost. All the time it was Mr God-almighty Shields Olsen ought to have been watching.

One thing was sure; once he reached the top of

the wash he'd have his revenge, on Shields, on the corporal with the cracked skull, the rabbit-faced private.

One more yard. You can do it.

He sank clawed fingers into the slope and pulled himself upwards dragging his face above the lip of the wash. He wedged his chin on the lip, gouged one shoulder into a soft pocket of sand, dug in his toes. He hung there. After a time, after his eyes got used to the sun glare, he made out the country ahead, the rope corral and tents and timber along the creek. He saw figures, two of them in blue uniform. Anger worked in him and he thought about his revenge.

There was a movement in the corner of his eye, he twisted his head. He saw in the sky above him, two buzzards drifting. He thought, just stay up there, you bastards, and I'll give you another, bigger meal than me ... who else could have done that, climbed the wash, lugging a rifle....

Where was the rifle?

For a minute he thought he'd let the weapon slide back into the wash and felt terror, despair; then he saw the Remington wedged against the side of the wash, level with his knees. All he had to do was reach down for it. He'd put too much burnish on the barrel; it hurt his eyes looking at it. He reached down, conscious of pain building in his stomach ... he knew then he wasn't going to have his revenge after all, Shields had killed him, or left him a cripple, which would be even worse, he had no feeling in his legs. But I'll kill you first, he told Shields, if I can only reach this rifle and lift it....

His fingers touched the walnut of the Remington. In the same instant the pain came, crashing through him like a dark wave. He wanted to scream but he couldn't. The sky turned the colour of rust and he felt a new wash of sweat. The pain changed, now it jolted through him, each jolt worse than the last. He thought, you ain't gonna kill me, Shields, not until I've killed you. And then he couldn't think of anything, there was nothing but pain, no past or future beyond the pain in his body, no revenge, no remorse ... only the rusting sky, now the colour of old blood, now a red-black void ... and his fingers, hinged into claws of agony, hooked about the stock of the Remington....

The corporal slipped the noose about Taylor's neck. He made and lit a cigarete and gave it to the prisoner.

Powers tamped and relit his pipe. He told the captive, 'I don't know if you are a student of history, Mr Taylor. But you are an interesting specimen, from a historical perspective.'

Shields said, 'Let's get on with it, for God's sake!'

Powers waved the hand that held the pipe. 'Just let me say this. The situation you find yourself in, Mr Taylor ... why? Could it be you've been too good at your job?.'

'How'd you figger that?'

Powers smiled. 'Let's put it this way. You've used your virtually unique abilities to hunt down red savages, to discourage outlawry. You have largely succeeded. Yet don't you see, Taylor, that your success is bound to be your undoing? You're like a fish imbibing the water it swims in. As the country becomes what you've made it – settled, civilized, organized – men like yourselves, at the very cutting edge, the knife point as it were, of civilization, themselves become anachronisms. Become as undesirable to forward-looking Arizonans as the Indians or bandits you've eliminated. You have an unsavoury reputation, Mr Taylor. Despite the valuable contribution you've made, you are rewarded with dislike and distrust throughout the territory. Isn't that so? Such is very often the case, I know myself ... also your reputed preference for dusky savage maidens....'

Powers spent a moment getting his pipe going again. He went on: 'You provided a sort of justice once, I'll grant. But your justice makes each man his own judge, jury and executioner. It is unacceptable once an alternative form of law arrives. Even that sordid policeman, what'shisname, Olsen, at least there was a place for him in the new scheme of things. But your day is passing. What happens to you now is what would have happened to you eventually, at the hands of so-called respectable citizens ... what always happens to those who outlive their time and usefulness.'

Shields said, 'It's like you dirty up the territory.'

Taylor snorted. '*I* dirty up the territory?'

Powers rubbed his two large hands together. 'As I said, civilization has come around you like a noose.'

Griffin took first place on the rope. Next the private. Third Shields. Powers hauled off his frockcoat, took his place as anchorman. Shields and Powers looked strong enough to lift a bull, just the two of them.

Powers asked, 'Have you any last words, Taylor?'

Taylor stared off into the distance, north-east towards the nearest mountains. What words could say it? What words could make sense of this way of dying? He'd been on the wrong trail from the start, after Olsen when the real villains were right under his nose. What could make that right?

No, all he had was the past. A dozen different landscapes, long-vanished friends, faceless women. Ma, long dead, Pa, maybe still alive for all he knew, or cared; men he'd killed, old pain, old wounds ... Nah-Lin in that faded blue settler's blouse she liked to wear ... little Nachay, asleep on his mother's back, tiny fingers hinged around the rim of the cradle-board. Two graves under the Mazatzal snow ... he couldn't feel sad, he could only feel angry, at his captors, at the wrongness of this.

Shields told his companions, 'When I say pull....'

Maybe no one could make a mark big enough to last on this landscape, Taylor thought. Maybe all that mattered was the land ... he looked at the desert sky, cloudless, stunning blue, the trembling whiskers of a honey mesquite, the nooning sun setting fire to the land, mountains, rocks and shrubs, sparkling like a crystal chain ... a rock, over there, under the slow wheel of buzzards, star-gleaming like a jewel or burnished metal. No, words weren't big enough, there weren't any words.

Powers spat on his hands, gripped the rope and braced his great shoulders for the pulling. He asked, 'Have you any last words, Taylor?'

The range detective sneered, 'I figgered you'd never quit talking, Powers.'

Shields called, 'Pull!'

Powers fell backwards. As he fell, he let go of the rope, so the others staggered, the corporal went to one knee.

At first, Taylor thought Powers had just stumbled; then he heard the shot.

The private released the rope and sprang backwards, pulling his belt gun; there was another shot, he went to his knees, toppled on his side; the pistol fell from his hand.

Shields and Griffin let the rope fall. There was a third shot and both men ducked, lunging into the brush.

Taylor loosened the rope, he threw the noose over his head and dived for the pistol the private had dropped. He got the weapon. Lifting his head, he saw Shields, halfway to cover, undecided as to whether to keep going or to finish Taylor first; he swung around, facing the range detective, lifting his gun as Taylor did the same. They fired together. The rancher staggered, one hand to his side, sat on his rump. Griffin also veered from cover, his carbine half-raised; Taylor saw the muzzle swing around towards his chest. He lifted his pistol again, cocked and fired. Griffin's right leg was knocked from under him and he went down in dust. He lifted to one elbow and Taylor shot him in the chest and in the throat. After that, the Texan kicked a little.

There seemed to be a long time when nothing happened. A long silent time when no guns sounded. Wearily, Taylor got to his feet. He half expected the hidden rifle to seek him out too, but no more shots came.

Powers sat, smiling contentedly; the faces of the other dead men were contorted in their final agonies. Taylor said, 'Your friends is dead, Shields.'

Shields glared. He lifted a bloody hand from his side and swore. Taylor saw his gaze move on a little, to a Colt pistol lying in the dust, two yards from his outstretched foot.

Taylor said, 'Why don't you try for it?' He found